"We need to talk. Privately."

Nick's voice resonated inside Billie like a gust of warm air. His hot gaze traced every curve from the round of her breast to the indentation of her waist and swell of her hips. No one had ever looked at her as Nick did now. It unraveled her composure. It made her jittery. But it also gave her a smug confidence she'd never experienced. She'd always known she could ride or rope as well as any cowboy. But she'd never known she could turn a man's head.

"Fine, I'll show you the ranch." Maybe he'd be impressed. He'd see her as a strong-willed woman who could run a ranch and marry any man she pleased.

"And we'll talk," he warned.

Terrific, Billie thought, just what she needed—a heart-to-heart with the man who'd unknowingly stolen hers.

Dear Reader,

Traditionally June is the month for weddings, so Silhouette Romance cordially invites you to enjoy our promotion JUNE BRIDES, starting with Suzanne Carey's *Sweet Bride of Revenge*. In this sensuously powerful VIRGIN BRIDES tale, a man forces the daughter of his nemesis to marry him, never counting on falling in love with the enemy....

Up-and-comer Robin Nicholas delivers a touching BUNDLES OF JOY titled *Man, Wife and Little Wonder*. Can a denim-clad, Harley-riding bad boy turn doting dad and dedicated husband? Find out in this classic marriage-of-convenience romance! Next, Donna Clayton's delightful duo MOTHER & CHILD continues with the evocative title *Who's the Father of Jenny's Baby?* A woman awakens in the hospital to discover she has amnesia—and she's pregnant! Problem is, *two* men claim to be the baby's father—her estranged husband...and her husband's brother!

Granted: Wild West Bride is the next installment in Carol Grace's BEST-KEPT WISHES series. This richly Western romance pairs a toughened, taut-muscled cowboy and a sophisticated city gal who welcomes his kisses, but will she accept his ring? For a fresh spin on the bridal theme, try Alice Sharpe's *Wife on His Doorstep*. An about-to-be bride stops her wedding to the wrong man, only to land on the doorstep of the strong, silent ship captain who was to perform the ill-fated nuptials.... And in Leanna Wilson's latest Romance, *His Tomboy Bride*, Nick Latham was *supposed* to "give away" childhood friend and bride-to-be Billie Rae—not claim the transformed beauty as his own!

We hope you enjoy the month's wedding fun, and return each and every month for more classic, emotional, heartwarming novels from Silhouette Romance.

Enjoy!

Joan Marlow Golan

Joan Marlow Golan
Senior Editor Silhouette Romance

Please address questions and book requests to:
Silhouette Reader Service
U.S.: 3010 Walden Ave., P.O. Box 1325, Buffalo, NY 14269
Canadian: P.O. Box 609, Fort Erie, Ont. L2A 5X3

HIS TOMBOY BRIDE

Leanna Wilson

Silhouette

ROMANCE™

Published by Silhouette Books

America's Publisher of Contemporary Romance

For Gary,
the best husband in the world!

Acknowledgments

As always, to my critique buds—Alyson, Betty and
Tammy. Much thanks goes to Frank Weatherford
(and Hawker Crane!).

 SILHOUETTE BOOKS

ISBN 0-373-19305-X

HIS TOMBOY BRIDE

Books by Leanna Wilson

Silhouette Romance

Strong, Silent Cowboy #1179
Christmas in July #1197
Lone Star Rancher #1231
His Tomboy Bride #1305

LEANNA WILSON,

a native Texan, was born and bred in Big D, but she's a country girl at heart. More at home dreaming up stories than lesson plans, she gave up teaching to pursue writing. Once she began putting her stories onto paper, it didn't take her long to publish her first Silhouette Romance novel, *Strong, Silent Cowboy*, which won the Romance Writers of America's Golden Heart Award. She's married to a strong, not-so-silent city slicker and lives in Lewisville, Texas, with their "children"—two lively shih tzus. She loves to hear from her readers. You can write to her c/o: Leanna Wilson, P.O. Box 294277, Lewisville, TX 75029-4277.

All underlined places are fictitious.

Chapter One

With a mixture of disbelief and wariness, Billie Rae Gunther stared at her wedding gown. The Italian satin looked like a collapsed bridal cake flung across her bedroom floor. How could she wear this frilly concoction? She'd look like a child playing dress-up instead of a beautiful, blushing bride.

"Be careful," Rosa warned. The dressmaker opened the gown and pushed the expensive material out of the way of Billie's feet. Nervous about the outcome of this folly, Billie pointed a silk-covered toe and stepped into the mounds of fabric to have the dress fitted. A tremor of apprehension rippled through her. What if she tore a seam? Worse, what if she looked like a fool?

Wiggling her hips, Billie settled into the waist and draped the satin across her shoulders. The cool cloth felt as slippery as the catfish she'd caught in Willow's Pond last fall. Feeling like a stuffed trout, she rocked back and forth from foot to foot.

"Hold still," Rosa admonished.

Billie sucked in a breath. It seemed to take hours instead of seconds as Rosa's nimble fingers fastened the long row of buttons along Billie's spine. Worried, she slanted her gaze toward the oblong mirror angled in the corner of her childhood room and watched the slow transformation. The creamy white material hugged her frame, and the lace gave her more curves than she owned, making her look softer and more feminine than her faded Wrangler jeans and scuffed Justin boots ever did. Hope swelled inside her. Maybe she could shed her tomboy image and be the woman she'd always imagined.

Then she caught sight of her V-necked tan line standing out in the middle of her chest like an inverted scarlet letter. A wave of apprehension rolled over her. She couldn't hide the fact she was a tomboy, a cowgirl, or good ol' "Billie the Kid." In the far recesses of her mind she heard Jake, her older brother, and his best friend, Nick, snickering and calling her that nickname. The memory brought a sharp, double-edged pain to her heart.

Rosa secured the veil across the top of Billie's head with hairpins, then stepped back. Satisfied with her creation, she beamed, her wide smile splitting her coppery face. "Ah, so beautiful!" Her solid black gaze narrowed and her brow withered into a frown. "Why this face?" She lifted Billie's chin a notch. "Why so sad?"

Billie shrugged. "I'm okay. I was thinking about Jake and…" She stopped, shaking her head, trying to shrug off her sorrow like a pesky injury. But this ache wouldn't go away. He'd been too young, too foolish driving his truck hell-bent for leather. She couldn't think about her brother now. Nor would she think about Nick Latham. His memory would bring a different kind of pang. He'd moved out of Bonnet, Texas, and on with his own life…without her.

No longer a kid with fanciful dreams, she was a full-grown woman of twenty-three. She drew in a confident breath and adjusted the material bunching around her shoulders. How difficult could parading around like a Barbie doll be? It couldn't be harder than running her daddy's ranch, juggling the finances or marrying a man she didn't love.

Responsibility constricted her like the dress tried to cut off her circulation above her waist. She never could stay ahead of the demands on her time or bank account. Her father's sudden death five years ago had heaped half the responsibility on her narrow shoulders. In his will, he'd left Billie and Jake the ranch, knowing their mother would never be able to take care of it on her own. Two years later Jake's death had left her with a barnyard of unexpected debts and *all* the responsibility. Now, her desperation, her determination, had brought her to this—her wedding.

Reality had a sharper edge and required practical decisions. This marriage solved a truckload of problems for her. She'd face her future with the same grit that had helped her through each tragedy in her life. This time, the things she cared about wouldn't be taken away from her. This time, she'd take the reins in her own hands and guide her own destiny.

Marriage didn't come wrapped up in a nice, neat package with frilly ribbons and bows. Billie would not risk her heart on her fiancé or anyone else. She'd tried that once. And failed. With deep scars as proof, she'd learned once too often that love hurt. She could do without any more pain.

Rosa sniffed. "Too much sorrow for one family. Let us think of your wedding. Put on your shoes and come. Let's not keep your mother waiting."

Ignoring the satin pumps that looked about as comfortable as the strapless underwire bra she wore beneath her dress, Billie pulled her fancy white boots out of the closet. She hadn't worn these since she'd gone boot-scootin' in high school. At least the boots were comfortable.

She left her bedroom, lifting the heavy skirt out of the way, the lush satin brushing against her legs and rustling with each step. She moved past framed pictures of family vacations in the Rocky Mountains, her and Jake huddled in front of a tilted Christmas tree, and school pictures chronicling Billie's blackened eyes, pigtails and braces. The fond memories fortified her with the courage she needed to face her future.

"Here comes the bride!" Martha Gunther sang, her voice warbling like an old-fashioned organ. Her face crinkled with a warm smile. Her blue eyes sparkled with unshed tears.

Feeling less like a bride and more like a trussed up heifer, Billie waddled into the den. Shoulders back, she gave her mother her best, most optimistic smile, the same one she used after she paid each month's bills and counted the leftover money in the checking account.

A movement in the corner of the living room caught her eye. She squinted against the afternoon sunlight pouring through the bay window across the front of her parents' house. The tall, dark, masculine frame had broad shoulders and a height that would put most men to shame. Her breath caught in her lungs. Had Doug, her fiancé, come early? Maybe the light distorted his size, making him larger than his normally slight, elegant build. Her groom shouldn't be seeing her wedding dress. It was bad luck. And that was one thing she didn't need any more of.

"Billie the Kid?" The warm, deep, masculine voice jolted her like a bolt of electricity.

Her breath whooshed out of her. For a second she felt dizzy, her world tilting off center. *Nick!*

Nicholas Barrett Latham stepped toward her, effectively blocking the sun slanting through the window behind him. She met his gold-flecked amber gaze. Something warm and uncomfortable, something she hadn't experienced in years, stirred inside her. He ran his fingers through his thick chestnut hair. A grin split his chiseled, tanned features and zapped the strength right out of her knees.

"Well," he said, rubbing his hand against his square jaw, "I'll be damned."

Nick wasn't her groom, but he was bad luck, all right. She wished her dress would swallow her whole and bury her beneath the yards of lace and satin. So help her, if he laughed at her in this dress, she'd deck him. In anticipation of having to do just that, her hands curled into fists.

"Isn't it wonderful for Nick to visit us, honey?" her mother said, hugging her own middle as if she might burst with excitement.

Billie nodded automatically. For once in her life words failed her. Or maybe for the second time. The first had been when she'd kissed Nick. She'd grown up since that hot summer day when she'd been a naive sixteen-year-old. But with Nick's irresistible smile and curious gaze settling on her now, her insides felt mushy once again, like jelly left out of the refrigerator for too long.

"I heard you were getting married," he said in a rumbling voice that made her stomach roll. "Had to see it for myself."

His surprise ruffled her feathers. She met his intense

gaze squarely. "Why? Is it so impossible to believe someone would want me?"

"I didn't mean...I... No. 'Course not.'" His features twisted with confusion. He stepped forward and awkwardly brushed a kiss against her cheek. "Congratulations, Billie."

The warmth of his lips sent a surge of heat through her body. She drew in a quick, inadequate breath. Nick stood so close she could have touched him if she'd dared. She smelled his clean, spicy scent, which reminded her of the sharpness of cedar after a summer rain. Her voice caught on the words, "Welcome home, Nick."

His hand slid around her cinched-in waist and pulled her close against his chest. She felt the hardness of his muscles, the strength in his arms, the gentleness of his words as his breath warmed her ear. "It's good to see you again, Billie."

His solid embrace made her feel weak as a newborn colt. She stepped back on the hem of her dress. To her chagrin, Nick steadied her with a hand under her elbow. Her heart hammered in her chest. Her breath came hard and fast, as if she'd run up a steep hill.

"How long has it been?" she asked, knowing it had been exactly two years, one month and sixteen days. She didn't ask herself how she knew or why. She didn't want to question whether it was because she so clearly remembered the cool, rainy spring day when she'd stood at her brother's graveside or because Nick had been there.

"Too long," he answered.

Knee-deep in grief at her brother's funeral, Billie remembered Nick's fierce hug, an awkward pat on her shoulders, a gruff, "I'm so sorry, Billie." She'd been unable to restrain the resentment at seeing his pretty wife standing beside him. Maybe that's why she'd been so damned determined to handle the Rocking G Ranch on her own. If she couldn't have Nick's love, then by God she'd have his respect. That's why he couldn't know she was selling out now...to marriage.

So much had changed since that rainy day. Regret swept through her. She alone bore the guilt of why Nick hadn't visited the Gunthers since his best friend's funeral. Instinctively she sensed Nick had changed, too. Something in his face, his eyes. A harder glint had replaced the mischievous glimmer of his youth. Feeling his gaze on her like a warm caress, her dress suddenly felt tight, the air thin, her blood thick as molasses.

"We all should have kept in touch," Martha said, "after Jake..." She shook her head.

Sorrow darkened Nick's eyes to a deep walnut.

After Jake's funeral he'd offered to stay and help with the ranch, but Billie had wanted—needed—to prove she could handle it as well as any man. But she hadn't known about the money Jake had borrowed. She hadn't known a lot of things then. It had been an uphill battle ever since to stay in operation.

Martha patted Nick's arm as if he was her own son. "We've missed you."

"I was negligent," he said, his voice thick. "I should have come back sooner."

Billie lifted her chin and met his questioning gaze. "We managed fine. We didn't need any help."

And we don't need anything now.

A wry chuckle escaped his tense mouth. "You always could take care of things."

Her heart lurched. She hadn't managed very well with the ranch. Good ol' Billie Rae—strong, capable, dependable—she'd always prided herself on her good qualities.

But did they really describe her or a well-bred stock horse?

Irritated at her own comparison, she wanted to believe Nick's words were a compliment. But in her heart they taunted her. For a moment she wished she could melt into a helpless puddle of tears instead remaining stoic and practical in the face of adversity. But she hadn't. She couldn't.

More than ready for him to leave, she asked, "What brings you back here?"

"You." Something suggestive in his tone made her toes curl under.

"Me?" Her voice squeaked.

With the swiftness of summer lightning, she remembered the burning intensity of their one shared kiss, the awareness sparking between them, the heat searing her to her very feminine core. The texture of his mouth, firm yet gentle, as rough and tempting as raw silk, had awakened her like Prince Charming had stirred Sleeping Beauty from sleep. She had suddenly been proud of her softer curves, grateful finally that she was a girl… woman.

At sixteen she'd suffered a bad case of puppy love. But it had been more, she'd realized as time had passed, as she'd matured, as the feelings had lingered and intensified. It had been real, true. From the very depths of her soul. She'd wanted to marry Nick, have his children. Loving him had outshone all her other dreams. When hit with his captivating gaze, she'd have done anything for him. Then he'd splintered a small part of her heart.

So she'd focused with laser beam precision on her hopes of becoming a vet. It hadn't taken long for that dream to crash beneath the weight of her father's death and be buried beneath the burden of her brother's. Years of hard, backbreaking work and shoulder-scrunching responsibility had demolished the rest of her innocent hopes. Once she'd had grand plans for her life. None of them had come to pass. But she hadn't given up on all of them yet.

As abruptly as she'd been set back on her heels that day when Nick had told her of his impending marriage, now again she pulled herself up short from her steamy memories. She reminded herself with a quick mental kick that she didn't want Nick. She had other plans, plans that resurrected her dreams. Plans that didn't include him.

The cold, wet glass cooled the skyrocketing temperature that burned inside him like a high-pitched fever. Nick felt hotter than the hundred-degree weather outside. He sipped the sweetened tea, and the ice clinked together. The ceiling fan sifted cool air over his heated skin.

Wedding! He still couldn't believe it. Billie the Kid was *really* getting married. His world turned upside down as if E no longer equaled mc^2. He felt the foundation under him collapsing.

But Nick couldn't concentrate on anything except Billie. And her vibrant blue eyes. Her golden hair teased her smooth, bare shoulders and made him think of things he didn't ordinarily associate with Billie, like satin sheets on hot summer nights. Her faint tan line, outlining the opening of a work shirt, brought a smile to his heart as he remembered the rough-and-tumble girl she'd once been. And now she was all grown-up.

For the first time he noticed her very distinctive, patently feminine and too-damn-sexy curves. His "kid sister" had become a woman. A part of him was more than grateful there wasn't an ounce of blood relation between them.

His throat went bone-dry. He coughed, uncomfortable with his blatant, sexually charged reaction to her. "Tim Cummins told me your good news. I ran into him yesterday in Houston."

One part of the rumor had been true enough. But he still held out hope the rest had been false.

"We should have called," Martha said, "but it's been so rush-rush, with all the plans and everything." She touched a trembling hand to Billie's veil. "I wish your father could see you like this. He would have been so proud." She turned away and sniffed again into her handkerchief.

Billie's features contorted, the muscles along her neck flexing. Nick wondered if her father's absence took away part of her wedding joy. Mr. Gunther wouldn't be there to walk her down the aisle or twirl her around the dance floor. Didn't a woman want that emotional support, those tender moments?

None of the Gunther men were alive to offer guidance to Billie. Nick knew neither of them would approve of the groom Tim Cummins had said won Billie's hand. Nick wouldn't, either. It had to be some mistake. The Billie he knew would be more discerning than that. That's why he'd dropped everything, including work, and raced back to Bonnet—to make sure she knew what she was doing.

She met his gaze. A sparkle glinted in her eyes, making them look as dazzling as sapphires. One minute she looked childlike—lost, alone, bereft—and the next, she appeared ready to take on the world. Billie had always surprised him with her quick-flash change of emotions. What the hell did he know about women, anyway? They were an enigma. His divorce was a blatant reminder.

She broke the fragile silence with, "Jake would have gotten a good belly laugh about all this."

Something familiar and warm passed between them, but a new spark ignited, something disconcerting and way too hot. Ignoring his very male reaction to her obvious feminine charms, he matched her smile with an unsteady one of his own. "You're right. He would have."

Then her eyes flashed. Her smile faltered. She tipped her chin higher. He recognized that old challenge.

Jake might have laughed at her all dressed up like this. But Nick couldn't. His lungs constricted, trapping his breath. Words lodged in his throat. She looked so damn different...so grown-up...so beautiful. When had all these changes taken place? At her father's funeral five years earlier she'd looked like a frightened child, her eyes wide, but unable to shed a tear. At Jake's funeral two years later, she'd looked thin as a rail. She'd stood strong for her mother, brave, controlling her trembling lip.

He'd missed the gradual transition from girlhood to a full-fledged woman. Somehow she seemed softer than he'd expected, vulnerable, yet he knew she was tough enough to handle a Texas cattle ranch on her own. Still, a trace of that uncertain, freckle-faced girl could still be seen in her wild, blue gaze.

"Jake would have been a fool not to see how beautiful you are," he managed.

Uncertainty darkened her eyes to the turbulence of a stormy sea. She glanced down at the yards of lace swirling around her. "I feel like I got walloped with confectioners' sugar."

Nick chuckled.

"You're a lovely bride," Martha reassured her daughter.

"Lovely" was a simple word that didn't do Billie justice. She was a vision. The dress pinched in her waist, accented her full breasts, showed off her honey tan.

As if the years scrolled backward, he remembered the boldness of the kiss she'd given him. He could feel her creamy-smooth lips seasoned with innocence brushing his. It had taken every ounce of strength to set her away from him then. He'd belonged to someone else. And Billie had been way too young. But now, when the four-year difference between their ages had shrunk in importance, other things stood between them. *She* belonged to someone else. *He* never intended to marry again.

Dragging his gaze away from the bride, he set the iced tea on a crystal coaster. He stuck his hands into his pockets and reminded himself of why he'd come here. As a defensive maneuver, he pictured Billie in pigtails and braces with more scrapes and bruises than a prizefighter.

"Step up on the footstool," Rosa instructed, her hands fluttering around the shimmering white skirt that looked like it had been sprinkled with fairy dust.

Billie turned and took a step. Her foot caught in the hem. She wobbled and tilted off center. Her arms flung wide, seeking balance. "Ah, damn."

Nick reached out and caught her to him. His hand slipped around her tiny waist. Her body collided with his. He felt the impact of her full breasts against his chest. He sucked in a breath and drew in her enticing scent, something mysterious and exotic, like jasmine. Far too tempting for his own good.

A shiver rippled through her and it echoed in his body. His heart thudded against his rib cage. His insides tightened as if he walked an I-beam on the fiftieth floor. These new sensations aroused by Billie caught him off guard, kept him off balance. Her nearness jumbled his thoughts.

What was wrong with him? Had he gone without a woman for too long? Since his divorce he'd focused on work, expanding his construction business. Women, he'd decided, were as welcome as bad weather to a construction site. And Billie Rae Gunther was like a hurricane to his senses.

He had an urge to let her fall on her rump, as he might have if she were an obnoxious twelve-year-old. Then he could clear his mind, stay focused, make sure she'd made the right decision and leave. Instead, against his better judgment, he held her tight against him, his hands secure on her waist. In a thick voice, he asked, "You okay?"

"Yeah. My boot got caught." She pushed away from his shoulder and stood firmly on her own two feet, the way she always had, never leaning on anyone, never showing any weakness. She carried the heavy load of responsibility she'd been left with well. Nick admired her for her ability to withstand adversity.

Two years ago he'd understood her pride dictated her rejection of his offer to help with the Rocking G. But should he have insisted? Or had he only felt the barb that she no longer needed or wanted him? Regret shamed him. He knew he shouldn't have stayed away.

"Boots! Where are your wedding shoes? They are perfect for the dress," Rosa was saying, her brow wrinkling with concern.

"Yeah, but you don't have to stand around in them for hours at the wedding and reception," Billie complained.

"It's only for one day." Martha soothed her daughter. "The right shoes are so important."

"Why?" Billie asked. "Who's going to see them under this skirt?" She lifted the hem, giving Nick a glimpse of one silk-covered foot rubbing across the top of the other.

"Everyone," her mother answered. "You'll have to lift your skirt so Doug can remove your garter to throw to the single men."

Nick gritted his teeth. *Doug.* It had to be a mistake. The groom couldn't be Doug "Blockhead" Schaeffer!

"Besides," Martha continued, "you'll have so many other things to think about you won't even notice your feet. You'll be floating on cloud nine. That's how I was when your daddy and I wed." A wistful look came into her soft blue eyes.

"I'm sure I will, Mother."

Had Nick heard a note of doubt in Billie's voice? Or had he only wanted to?

Scowling, he watched her maneuver toward the step stool in her oversize skirt. The heavy material rustled and swayed, emphasizing the movement of her hips. He stayed close enough to offer assistance if she tripped again, but far enough not to breathe in her secretive scent or reach out to feel the silky strands of her shoulder-length blond hair. Hiking up the skirt to her knees, she climbed onto the footstool, unassisted. Nick caught a better view of shimmery hose covering slender legs.

"Who's the lucky groom?" he asked, averting his gaze and crossing his arms over his chest.

"Doug Schaeffer."

Something irrational and dangerous exploded inside Nick. He thought he'd prepared himself to hear that name, but obviously not enough. "Are you nuts?"

She propped her hands on her hips and gave him a stubborn I-dare-you-to-say-another-word stare. "Yes."

He managed to close his mouth and rein in his confusion…irritation…contempt. How could Billie possibly fall for that bastard? What could she see in him? Of all the men to win Billie! Smug and arrogant were two of Doug's *best* traits. The heir to Schaeffer Enterprises should never have been a contender.

He remembered Doug, flaunting his daddy's bucks, cruising around in a fancy convertible that probably had the same price tag as the house Nick had been raised in. He'd been too rich for his own good, too self-assured, too...too much. Had he overwhelmed Billie with all that glitter and gold? If so, then Billie wasn't the girl he remembered. Maybe now she was more like his ex-wife.

"Where is Schaeffer?" Nick asked, his teeth clenched. Billie's father never would have welcomed Schaeffer into the family. And Jake would have booted his butt across the Texas border. Nick would settle this quick and take great pleasure in shoving Schaeffer out of the picture.

"Oh, the groom should not be here to see the bride dressed in her gown." Rosa shook her head. "Very bad luck."

"Better than if Schaeffer saw her *un*dressed," Nick mumbled, his scowl deepening.

Rosa and Martha paid no attention to him. They concentrated on tucking and pinning pieces of the dress to Billie's long, lithe form.

He wondered then if the bride and groom had been...intimate, if Schaeffer had held Billie, naked in his arms. A cold clamp tightened around Nick's spine. He ground his teeth at the idea of Doug Schaeffer touching Billie, kissing her, making love to her. A headache twisted through his skull like steel screws digging into his scalp.

"Doug's working," Billie answered. The healthy glow across her cheeks brightened and made Nick imagine her lips swollen from kisses, her skin flushed, her hair tousled from lovemaking.

His hands balled into fists. "Work was never in Schaeffer's vocabulary."

"He's running Schaeffer Enterprises." Irritation made her snap the words. She crossed her arms over her chest, pushing her breasts higher until the soft mounds almost spilled out of the scooped neckline.

"I bet old man Schaeffer's still pulling the strings." Nick turned and drained the glass of iced tea as if it was a shot of whiskey. Unfortunately, it didn't have the same numbing effect.

"Didn't your father start that construction company you run, Nick?" Billie taunted.

Her barb hit its mark. He swung around to throw back another sharp retort, but her smug look killed it on his lips. He wouldn't give her the satisfaction.

Martha uncrossed her daughter's arms so the dress would hang right. Rosa clucked her tongue and examined the hem.

"I didn't have any choice," he said finally, his voice cracking with suppressed anger. "My dad needed me. There were contracts pending, signed agreements that had to be met. Dad was injured. He didn't have anyone to rely on...but me." Billie had to understand that kind of responsibility. She'd done the same with the ranch. "Doug works for his daddy because he *can't* do anything else."

"How would you know?" Billie's jaw squared in that old familiar way.

"You two," Martha grumbled, pins stuck between her teeth. "Sounds like old times."

"Then why doesn't Doug do whatever he wants?" Nick asked, ignoring Billie's mother.

"He is." Billie smirked. "He's marrying me."

Touché. The muscles along Nick's shoulders tensed, pinching the nerve endings like steel clamps. Her quick defense of Doug showed Nick he'd have to take another course. Irritating her wouldn't help. Stroking his chin as Billie's father had often done when confronted with one of his kid's problems, Nick said, "What are Doug's big plans for the future? Live off his healthy trust fund? Then what?"

"He has... *We* have plans. Lots of them. But I don't see that it's any business of yours, Nick Latham. You're not my father...or brother." Her voice deepened, a husky quality emphasizing her turbulent emotions. "You're not even family."

That hit another nerve. A raw one.

As if he'd taken a direct right hook to the jaw, he stepped back. His gaze locked with Billie's. In that moment he knew she was a grown woman, capable of making her own decisions and mistakes. He'd have to let her make this one on her own. But he didn't have to stay and watch.

"Billie Rae Gunther," Martha snapped, "you apologize this minute."

Nick met Billie's gaze, saw the regret, the pain inside her reflecting his own. He hadn't come here to argue. He'd come to help a girl who'd once been like a little sister. But that person no longer existed.

"She doesn't have to." He stepped toward the woman who'd been like a mother to him. "Billie's right. I'm intruding." He gently kissed the older woman's cheek. "I'll come back later. Before the weekend's over. So we can catch up."

Shaking her head, Martha bent and pinned another part of Billie's hem. "It's just like when y'all were kids.

Bickering and carrying on. How did Jake ever put up with the two of you?''

"He didn't," Billie said.

Nick caught the mischievous look in her eye and tension eased out of his body like air out of a balloon. "That's right. He used to lock you in the barn."

"Or toolshed," she added with a tight laugh.

"Not a bad idea." Maybe he'd give it a try. Let her stew until she came to her senses. Tempted to do just that, he wondered who would let her out now. He'd once been her rescuer. Not anymore. Was Schaeffer her knight in shining armor? His gut tightened. Schaeffer had never thought of anyone but himself. Shaking off his anger and concern, Nick reminded himself that Billie wasn't his responsibility. She never had been.

With a soft, reluctant sigh, he turned away.

"Nick…" The soft lilt of Billie's voice caught him off guard. He heard the rustle of her dress and a soft curse.

Turning back, he watched her hobble toward him.

Chagrin darkening her eyes to a deep blue, she said, "I'm sorry. You *are* family. It's just been a long time since we've seen you. And the wedding has me all stirred up."

Martha nodded. "Very emotional."

Billie rolled her eyes and compressed her lips into a thin line. Had she matured more than he'd thought? Billie the Kid had never refrained from saying anything that was on her mind or in her heart. But she'd never cried. Not even when she'd fallen off a horse and separated her shoulder. She'd never apologized, either. Not even when she'd run away from home at the age of seven and scared the living daylights out of her family…and Nick.

Instead of relying on tears, she'd fought tooth and nail. She'd buried her emotions at her father's funeral, acting brave and strong for her mother. He'd seen the need to grieve at her brother's burial. But again, she'd suppressed it. Maybe falling in love had tapped into those hidden emotions, pulling them loose and helping her reach her full potential as a woman.

But with Doug Schaeffer? He held his tongue. This wasn't the time or place to challenge Billie about her choice of a groom. He'd spoken out of turn earlier. What would he have said if someone had bad-mouthed his bride? Actually, he wished someone had. It would have saved him a load of grief. But he wouldn't have listened then, and he doubted Billie would listen now.

"I understand," Nick said. "I've got bad timing." *As usual.*

"No, it's fate." Martha's cheeks dimpled and her gaze shifted between Nick and the bride-to-be. "You are the answer to my prayers. We need you to help us with the wedding."

Great. He wanted no part of it. But how could he refuse? His love and concern for the Gunthers carved a deep groove in his heart.

"Whatever you need," he said, trying to manage a convincing smile. "What can I do?"

"Billie and I were discussing this just last week," Martha said. "Now that I think about it, you'd be perfect. Since you've been like a big brother to her and a son to me."

"Mother." Billie gave her a warning look. "What are you saying?"

Martha's gaze narrowed, then a grin split her face. "Nick, you should give away the bride."

Give her away? He stared first at Martha, then his gaze flicked to Billie. How could he give her away? When all he wanted was to keep her for himself.

That thought hit him like a demolition ball. He crushed it with common sense. He didn't want marriage, love or Billie the Kid Gunther. Keeping Billie for himself was a ridiculous notion. Marriage was not for him. Not anymore. Not since his had failed. His ex had made it abundantly clear that he didn't have what it takes to be married. He didn't understand the wants and needs of a woman. And he probably never would. He wouldn't risk his heart again.

But he could make sure Billie wasn't making a mistake. He owed Mr. Gunther and Jake that much. Before he left Bonnet, he'd make damn sure Billie loved Doug Schaeffer and vice versa. No matter how distasteful it seemed to Nick. For he knew the heartache of making the wrong choice. He wanted to spare Billie that much pain.

Giving away the bride gave him a responsibility...and maybe the excuse he needed to stay. Being a part of the wedding party would give him access to the bride and groom, to better evaluate if they were making the wrong decision. If they were, then he wouldn't hesitate to step in and break it up...as a big brother.

Chapter Two

Fat chance she'd let Nick Latham walk her down the aisle! Tension crackled in the silence following her mother's request. With an irritated flick of her wrist, Billie flung the veil off her shoulder. Her gaze collided with Nick's and started a chain reaction along her spine. She had to nip her mother's idea in the bud before it grew and took root. She couldn't let Nick give her away. Not in a million years!

She ignored the pesky, unrealistic notions popping up in her mind. Nick would not whisk her away and keep her for himself. That was ridiculous! He didn't want her. Not as a woman, anyway. He never had. And never would. She no longer wanted him, either. That had been a crazy childhood fantasy. Like other schoolgirl dreams, it had died.

Love hurts, she reminded herself. She wouldn't— couldn't—love Nick anymore. It was only seeing him again, his whiskey-colored eyes and easy smile, that had her so…unsettled.

Tiny pinpricks of awareness made each millimeter of her skin feel vibrant and alive. Her insides burned. Ignoring the hot sensations Nick aroused, she turned away from him and focused on the one person who could stop this insanity.

"Mother," Billie said, her voice rising with each pounding beat of her heart, "have you lost your mind?"

Her mother's smug smile dimmed. Her eyebrows arched in that familiar you've-gone-too-far maternal look. "No, I have not. And I don't appreciate your insinuation, young lady," Martha admonished. "I'm being very practical, just like you always are. After all, since your dear father passed away, I've spent long nights worrying about things like this. You need someone to escort you down the aisle."

"No, I don't." Billie planted her hands on her satin-covered hips. "I'm more than capable of walking myself down the aisle."

Her mother clucked her tongue. "That's just not done."

"Sure it is," Nick interrupted.

Martha's eyebrows slanted downward. Surprised he'd stood up for her, Billie cut her gaze toward him.

"Women do it all the time," he continued. "Last week, I attended a wedding in Houston. The bride's father had...well, not passed away, but he'd abandoned his family years before. The bride walked down the aisle by herself. She looked elegant and mature."

For once grateful for his presence, Billie perked up, liking his impressions of a lone bride proving her independence. "See, Mother?"

"It's disgraceful," Martha stated.

Rolling her eyes, Billie knew her romantic mother would never understand. "Poodle skirt" ideals remained fashionable in Bonnet, Texas. Martha would keel over in a dead faint if she knew Billie was marrying Doug for any reason other than love. If Nick knew, he'd probably jump on her mother's bandwagon, too. Which confirmed her conviction for keeping tight-lipped about her practical reasons.

Nick settled his hand on Martha's shoulder. "Billie should do whatever she chooses. After all, it's *her* wedding."

His words reassured her. She *had* made the right decision. Was Nick finally seeing her as a full-grown woman? The cocky slant of his eyebrow made her wonder. Maybe he was only looking for an excuse to get out of attending the wedding. Somehow that notion gave her an overwhelming sadness.

"Nick, honey—" Martha clutched at his arm "—I was counting on you to help me talk some sense into my daughter."

He patted her hand. His gaze shifted to Billie. His pointed stare put her back on the defensive. "Oh, I'm going to do just that."

His words held an ominous ring. What did he mean? Crossing her arms over her chest, she stood firm. She wouldn't let him derail her or her goal. She had plans for herself. Plans she'd waited a long time to fulfill. If Nick tried to stop her, she'd run right over him. She'd made up her mind. She'd chosen a mate—for better or worse.

"Why don't you finish with the dress fitting?" He nodded to Rosa who held her pincushion between her hands like a bouquet of delicate roses. "Billie and I can talk afterward. Privately."

His arrogant wink unnerved her. Whatever he had in mind, she'd beat him at his own game. For a moment she felt as if she were ten years old, trying to compete with her older brother and Nick. She'd had to work twice as hard, most of the time she'd relied on brains instead of brawn. This time wouldn't be any different.

But to best him, Billie needed to be on her own turf, not fumbling in a froufrou wedding dress in her mother's dainty parlor. She felt about as feminine as a tractor plowing down summer daisies. Her regular work clothes would give her the surefooted competence she needed.

With a confident tilt of her head, she said, "Fine, I'll show you the ranch."

If he saw the changes she'd implemented on the Rocking G, then he'd know for certain she could make well-thought-out, intelligent decisions. Maybe he'd be impressed. He'd see she wasn't a girl under the spell of puppy love. He'd see her as a strong-willed woman who could run a ranch and marry any man she damn well pleased.

"That's a good idea," he said.

His voice resonated inside her like a gust of warm air. His hot gaze traveled the length of her, tracing every curve from the round of her breast to the indentation of her waist and swell of her hips. Her body tingled with his lingering glance. Far more vulnerable in these layers of lace than she cared to admit, Billie longed for her denim jeans and muddy boots.

"She'll probably put you to work." Martha smiled and turned her attention to the satin trim along the bottom of the veil.

"I don't mind hard work." His rough, work-worn hands emphasized the truth of his statement. He gave Billie a mischievous grin that set her nerves on edge.

No one had ever looked at her as Nick did now. It unraveled her composure. It made her jittery. But it also gave her a smug confidence she'd never experienced.

She'd always known she could ride or rope as well as any cowboy. But she'd never known she could turn a man's head. Or was she only wishing she'd caught Nick's attention now?

"And we'll talk," he warned.

Terrific, Billie thought, just what she needed—a heart-to-heart with the man who'd unknowingly stolen part of hers.

Inside the barn, Nick inhaled the musty scent of baled hay and the sweet aroma of rolled oats. Memories assaulted his senses, reminding him of long days spent in the saddle...backbreaking workdays, happy days when Mr. Gunther would ask him to give Jake and Billie a hand with their chores. Those times seemed old and dim compared to the vibrant image before him. Billie walked out of a stall leading a sleek, chestnut quarter horse.

Even though she tried to hide the facts under an over-size plaid shirt, the evidence was clear—she was all woman. Her faded jeans hugged her slim hips as intimately as a man longed to hold a woman. The soft denim clung to her long legs and ended with frayed threads curling across well-worn black boots that boasted more cow manure and scratches than shine. With each step, she exuded confidence. He couldn't decide which way he liked her best—rough as an ordinary cowhand or elegant as any New York model. Or which wreaked more havoc on his libido.

"How long has it been since you've ridden horse-back?" Billie asked, a smirk tugging her lips into a half smile.

"High school, I guess," he said, leaning against a stall door where he'd draped his jacket. The warmth of the day had encouraged him to roll up the sleeves of his starched white shirt. "When Jake and I rode in that local rodeo. Remember? That was the day I knew I wasn't cut out for getting dumped in the dirt and stomped on like a rag doll."

Actually his dad's dream of handing the business over to him had been the deciding factor. It had been his dream, too. But it hadn't turned out the way he'd imagined.

"You decided you'd rather dig in the dirt?" A teasing smile pulled at her mouth.

"I let others do the digging. I'm the boss, remember?" His grin slowly faded with well-worn memories. "I always did like working with my dad, though."

He missed not being able to anymore. He'd always imagined them working side by side, building their construction company together. Tom Latham had retired and left his company entirely to his son's management. Sink or swim, it was up to Nick. Over the past five years his enjoyment had been squashed under the impact of reality. He'd liked working with his hands, building things, taking pride in his work. Now, running Latham Construction on his own kept him busy with management problems, obtaining permits, bidding on new contracts, handling employee relations. All the work and none of the fun.

"How is your dad?" she asked, her eyes full of interest and concern.

"Fine. Enjoying the easy life."

She nodded and turned back to her horse, smoothing her hand over the broad expanse of its back. "I remember your dad whooping and hollering for you at that rodeo," she said with husky warmth in her voice. "Didn't you get thrown?"

His shoulders snapped to attention. "Hell, who wouldn't have? That was a rank ol' bronc. If I recall,

Jake didn't fare so well, either. And your fiancé didn't even have the guts to try.''

"A real man doesn't have to ride a bronc to prove himself.''

"Ah, so that explains Schaeffer's…disinterest.'' Nick grinned.

She gave him a tight smile and slipped a snaffle bit into the horse's mouth, then slid a bridle over its head. Each movement shifted the unbuttoned plaid shirt and gave him a glimpse of the skimpier white cotton top beneath. The material stretched across her full breasts and lifted a notch to expose her smooth, flat stomach, which was two shades paler than her face and arms. His gut clenched tight as a Boy Scout knot.

Guilt lifted his gaze and urged him to give her an apology. But she didn't seem to notice him. Her attention was focused on the horse. She lovingly stroked the mare's nose. She had a way with animals. Her father had often entrusted her to care for scrawny calves that wouldn't nurse, and she'd turned them into big, strong beasts.

"I recall—'' Nick rubbed his jaw "—you were plenty interested in cowboys back then. Weren't you worried about me? Didn't you run out into the arena to see if I was all right?''

He remembered Billie rushing toward him as he lay in the dirt, his pride bruised as much as his backside. Fear had creased her brow, clouded her eyes. Embarrassment had pushed him onto his feet despite the pain in his knee. He'd brushed past her, trying to hide his limp.

Now, for some odd reason, a part of him longed for her to show some concern again. It made no sense. He didn't need her, any more than he needed anyone else.

Being near her unsettled him. Maybe he was simply feeling nostalgic, wishing for a simpler, easier time.

Her cheeks brightened to an enticing pink. She reached for a blue-and-green-plaid saddle blanket. "I was a silly schoolgirl then." One of her shoulders lifted as if she shrugged off the memory. "You were grumpy as an old bear, growling at me to leave you alone."

He chuckled. She'd cared about him once. Had those feelings faded like the blue in her jeans? Of course they had, he realized as disappointment pinched his already knotted gut. "No guy wants attention drawn to him when he's just landed on his rump in front of a hometown crowd. I wanted to lick my wounds in private."

"Well, trust me, if you get thrown today, I'll ignore you."

"No, you won't. You'll laugh."

"Maybe." She gave him a sly wink and laid the saddle blanket over the horse's back.

"You won't offer to kiss it and make it all better?" The words slipped out before he could stop them. They were a mistake. Instantly he regretted them, but he found himself holding his breath, watching her with more anticipation than he should have, waiting for her response.

Her eyes darkened like a cloud blotting out the sun. "I'm an engaged woman."

A wintry chill whipped through him. His face stiffened. He needed that reminder. He needed to get a firm handle on his feelings, his responsibilities. "What's the mare's name?"

Billie's eyes narrowed, then she looked at her horse. She nuzzled the side of the mare's neck. "Calamity."

He raised an eyebrow. "Is she a klutz? Or always causing trouble?"

Billie grinned, her white teeth flashing against her

honey-colored tan. "If there's a root snaking over the ground, she'll find it and trip. If there's a gopher hole, she's bound to step in it. She's been lucky not to hurt herself too badly. But she's great with rounding up calves. I don't know what I'd do without her."

He watched Billie's hands move over the horse in a loving, confident manner. He remembered how she'd cared for her father's animals, staying up late to help a colt enter the world, handling vaccinations deftly, crying when a sick kitten couldn't be saved. She had a tender heart. And he wouldn't let Doug Schaeffer trample it.

Billie flung a saddle over Calamity's back. Nick stepped to the side, bent and handed her the leather girth beneath. Their fingers brushed. His smile disappeared. With supreme effort, he clamped down on the desire to find out what it would feel like to hold her for real this time.

"You still remember which side to mount on?" she asked, humor lacing her words.

"Just give me a running start," he said, wondering if her mind swam with the same memories. Focusing on the past helped him picture the future. Billie was getting married—to someone else.

She glanced at him, a question lighting her eyes, then laughter burst out of her, the full, throaty sound stirring his interest again. "Oh, God, you remember that?"

"How could I forget you trying to ambush Jake and me like a Comanche on the warpath?"

Shaking her head, she grabbed the reins and headed out of the barn. "Come on, I'll saddle your mount."

"Which one am I riding?" he asked, stepping into the warm sunlight. The rays caught the gold shimmering highlights in Billie's blond hair and the intensity of her blue eyes.

"Diablo. You remember him, don't you?"

How could he forget Jake's surly black gelding that liked to kick and bite more than Billie the Kid? He nodded, wishing he'd brought his old rusted spurs. "Meanest bronc this side of the Red River."

Her mouth twitched as if she couldn't decide if she should smile. He figured she'd hold her laughter till he got thrown and busted his butt. She looped Calamity's reins loosely over a post, grabbed a rope and walked down the fence line. "Come on, we've got to catch him first. He's not very sociable these days."

When had Diablo ever been? Nick stuck his hands into his pockets. He was in for a long afternoon.

Billie whistled, and the shrill sound pierced the quiet barnyard. Birds fluttered toward their perches in the barn loft. In a nearby corral, a smattering of black cows and calves flinched. Diablo stood in the middle of a patch of green and chomped on sweet clover. Nick blinked. The once solid-black gelding was now gray, almost white in places.

Billie climbed the fence and jumped down into the corral. "He's hard of hearing, too."

"You sure it's safe to ride him?" Nick asked. "He looks...fragile."

"Don't let him fool you. He's stronger than he looks," she said, giving Nick a pointed stare. He caught her meaning. Billie was stronger than she looked, too, always had been. "Besides, Diablo likes the challenge."

Great, Nick thought. Wasn't Billie enough of a challenge for one day? He opened the gate for her to lead the gelding out of the corral. The horse acted as docile as an old hound. "You think you can race and win, with me riding this poor, pathetic excuse for a horse, huh?"

"No such thing." But she flashed him a devilish smile.

A few minutes later, mounted, they rode through a copse of live oaks and toward the green pastures. The horses' hooves crunched acorns as they walked. Nick's gaze trained on Billie, riding just ahead of him, as he rolled with Diablo's slower gait. The saddle cupped Billie's backside, framing her bottom, accenting the shifting motion of the horse. Nick groaned and concentrated on the thick green grass, the cornflower blue sky, the stark white fence surrounding the north stretch of the ranch.

"That a new fence?" he asked, noticing the rails where there used to be barbed wire.

She nodded. "Jake and I put that in right before..." Her voice faded, then she resumed. "It was expensive but in the long run it'll require less maintenance. And I don't have to worry about a cow breaking through and getting out onto the highway."

"Unless an eighteen-wheeler plows through it." He grinned, agreeing with her decision.

"Then I'd have more problems than an ornery cow on the loose."

"What are you going to do with the ranch once you get married?" he asked, prodding Diablo alongside the chestnut mare. Out of the corner of his eye, he detected the abrupt stiffening of Billie's spine.

"What do you mean?"

"I can't see Schaeffer letting his wife herd a bunch of smelly cows," he confessed, slanting his gaze to her face.

Her jaw squared, and her eyes flashed. "No man *lets* me do anything. It's *my* choice...whatever I do. With the Rocking G or anything else."

Her crisp tone signaled that the discussion was closed. He ignored the warning. "Are you selling out?"

"No." Her answer came quick. Too fast, almost defensive, in his opinion.

His eyes narrowed, but he couldn't read her expression. She shuttered her emotions behind a determined mask. "You've put a lot of blood, sweat and tears into this place. It's your heritage."

"I know that. Better than anyone." Her shoulders slumped as if beneath a great weight. "But…"

"What?"

She shook her head. "Nothing. We're keeping the ranch in the family. Doug can p-p—" She clamped her mouth closed and looked out over the north range.

He studied her for a long moment. "I didn't know you were unhappy here."

"There's a lot of things you don't know about me, Nick." She cut her eyes toward him. "How's the construction business these days?"

"Growing," he said, making a mental note that she hadn't denied she was unhappy.

"Do you like living in Houston?" Reining Calamity near a patch of clover, she draped her wrist over the saddle horn.

He shrugged as Diablo stopped to graze beside the mare, and turned in his saddle to look at her. "It offers a lot of opportunities."

"I would imagine so. For a single man." A faint tinge of pink brightened her cheeks. Her gaze softened. "We heard about the divorce, Nick. I'm sorry."

He tightened his grip on the reins. "So am I."

"Is marriage as hard as everyone says?" she asked.

"For me it was." Shifting on the hard saddle, he said, "Your mom would be a better one to ask. She made a marriage work for twenty some-odd years."

"But you know what it's like starting out in the nineties."

He set his mouth in a stern frown. "Yeah, it's hard."

He took the opportunity to drive home his point. "That's why it shouldn't be entered into lightly." He leaned toward her, until he was close enough to smell the musky scent that fogged his brain. "Level with me, Billie. You don't really love Doug Schaeffer, do you?"

She closed her fist over Calamity's reins and heeled her mount into a faster pace. "What do you mean?"

"You don't act like a blushing bride."

"Well, maybe because of the way you behaved earlier, I didn't think you wanted to hear me gush about my groom."

"That's probably true," he admitted, matching her stride.

A sudden need gripped him. A need to know she really didn't love Doug. For a split second he wondered if he was jealous, then dismissed it as concern—a feeling any big brother would have. "Tell me you're not going to marry him."

Her eyes narrowed. "We're engaged. The wedding date is set for one month from tomorrow."

"It's never too late. Not until you've said 'I do.'" Sadness softened his tone. He shook his head. "After all Doug's teasing. The way he used to pick on you. Why would you marry him? He's a jerk, Billie."

She squared her shoulders. "We were all jerky when we were young." She raised one brow. "Some of us outgrew junior high." She gave him a pointed stare. "Besides, Doug wasn't the only one who teased me."

He chuckled. "I see you haven't lost your backbone. That's a good sign. I teased you like a li'l sister. I wasn't mean. Not like Schaeffer."

"No," she admitted, her gaze softening. "You weren't mean."

"Now what can I say for you to break your engagement?" he asked, his voice low.

She jutted out her chin. "Doug and I are getting married."

"What can I *do*, then?" His voice dropped to a provocative tone as he remembered the kiss they'd once shared. His gaze shifted to her sensuous mouth. He stared at her full bottom lip, which looked ripe and plump as a summer strawberry. He remembered the softness of her lips, the warmth. His body tightened with renewed awareness. He jerked his thoughts upright. What had gotten into him? Had he lost his mind?

She turned in her saddle to face him. "You can't do a damn thing, Nick Latham. Go back to Houston...where you belong. And let me get married in peace."

Billie heeled her mount into a cantor, anger straightening her spine like a steel rod. What was Nick trying to do? Stop her wedding? Why was it so important to him?

Of course, she wouldn't let him. His pointed questions about the ranch stabbed at the raw guilt she already felt for failing to make it profitable. Nick was right; it was her heritage. But not her chosen path. She wanted to work with animals, but not breeding to sell them for somebody's juicy steak or cheeseburger. Each time she sold a truckload of cattle, her heart ached. She'd had to sell more recently to make ends meet. How much longer could she hold out? Her plan would keep the land in the family, provide a place for her mother to live, and give her the freedom to move on with her life. With Doug's money, she could hire someone to handle the ranch, and she'd oversee it as she went to school.

For some reason, though, she couldn't explain her feelings to Nick. He wouldn't understand. He'd made his father's business a success. And she didn't want his pity...or his contempt.

She wouldn't let him affect her, either. Although he already had. Far more than she cared to acknowledge. Her senses swirling, her mind spinning, she rode hard and fast until she noticed Calamity laboring for each breath. She reined in her mount and slowed to a trot then a walk. As her heart calmed to a steadier beat, she heard the rumbling sound of a horse approaching from behind. Knowing it was Nick, she kept her gaze straight ahead. She heard Diablo wheeze as Nick pulled alongside her.

"We better let Diablo rest," she said, swinging a leg behind her and dismounting. Once again, she'd overreacted, putting the gelding at risk. Guilt hung around her neck like a heavy yoke. She patted the old horse in a quiet apology.

Nick met her in front of the horses and looped the reins over Diablo's head. He watched Billie, but she ignored him. Her cheeks stung with an internal heat. Too aware of Nick, his stare, his smile, his broad shoulders that looked strong enough for a girl to rest her weary head upon, she broke off a sliver of knee-high grass and stuck the end between her teeth.

"Boy, I've missed this place. It feels like home." He led the horse through the field. "But it's changed."

Unsure of his tactics, she furrowed her brow. At least he'd chosen a safe topic. "A few months ago I built a new corral over near the swamp. Remember when Dad had us drag a feed trough over there to entice those wild heifers out of that pasture?"

"Yeah." He placed a hand on his lower back as if an old injury still pained him. "That she-devil kicked the slats out of me when I tried to herd her toward the truck."

"Well, now we have a feed lot with two troughs and

a chute. I can bring the cattle in, worm them, spray for flies or weed out any I plan to sell. I can herd one or two into the chute, then load them straight into the trailer from there.''

"Pretty smart," he said.

Relaxing a smidgen, she shrugged. "Well, I didn't come up with it all on my own. I saw Harold Jacobson with a similar operation. Do you remember ol' Mr. Jacobson? He used to teach the Ag courses at the high school. Dad and he were friends. And he's been generous with more agriculture advice since Jake and I started running things. He comes around about once a week to see how things are going." She smiled suddenly as if remembering something. "You had the hots for his daughter.''

Nick rubbed his jaw with his thumb as his mouth quirked with a fleeting smile. "I'd forgotten about her.''

Billie snorted and pursed her lips. "You always were the love-'em-and-leave-'em type. It was like a parade, watching the girls march in and out of your life. How many wore your letter jacket? Your class ring?''

"Ah, hell, Billie, I can't remember every girl I've ever dated. Can you remember every boy you ever went out with?''

Her jaws locked. Tension coiled around her like a snake. Of course, she could remember. There had only been one boy she'd ever wanted. And only one she'd ever dated. The first was standing beside her, staring at her as smug as any Neanderthal. The second was her fiancé.

"Can you?" he prompted, not letting her off the hook.

She kept her gaze trained straight ahead. "Yes, I can. Maybe I took dating a little more seriously than you did.''

"Why?" he asked.

She glanced at him, then wished she hadn't. He looked too damn sexy. Natural as any cowboy, he handled Diablo like a wrangler, not like her fiancé who looked like he'd rather be air-conditioned and sipping a Scotch. Squeezing off that thought, she walked faster.

"Because dating is…serious business. It has a purpose. To find the one you're going to marry. And I did." She reiterated her engaged state for her own sake as much as Nick's. When she looked at him, at the crinkles surrounding his hazel eyes, the tempting curve of his lower lip, she needed a clear reminder of why she'd chosen Doug instead of waiting for love.

"It's also to have fun. Didn't you ever date for fun?" His brow crunched into a frown.

Feeling the bite of resentment, she gritted her teeth. That was one more thing she'd never had time for. In fact, much to her chagrin, she'd never dated around period. Her experience with men had mostly been proving herself in a man's world. She'd preferred branding irons to curling irons. She hadn't cared about makeup or twittering gossip about the cutest boy. Unless it had centered on Nick.

He stopped walking and draped his arm over Diablo's withers. The reins dangled between his tanned fingers, drawing attention to his work-worn hands, which exuded strength, confidence and an amazing gentleness that she remembered from a long-ago caress.

"Didn't you ever go out with a man," he asked, "knowing you wouldn't marry him, and yet you had a damn good time?"

"No."

"You should before you get married," Nick said, his

tone serious. "You could go out with someone safe…a friend…like me."

"You? S-safe?" she sputtered.

"Sure." He rocked back on his heels. "I'm like your big brother. You couldn't be safer."

His hot gaze made her feel anything but.

"Just like that?" she quipped, her heart hammering its way into her throat. "What makes you think I'd go? That Doug would agree?" She doubted her fiancé would care if she went out with a friend, but she'd never wanted to date Nick…as a friend. And she didn't want to do so now.

"I thought you said no man *let* you do anything."

He'd caught her. His teasing smile pulled one out of her.

"So, are you gonna take me up on my offer?" he asked, his smile casual, his gaze intense.

Her mouth thinned into a tight line. "This won't work, Nick. I don't know if you're desperate or what, but I can't go out with you."

"Why?" His voice sounded smooth as silk.

She turned on him then. "Would you have let Diane date while y'all were engaged?"

He rubbed his jaw. "I wish now that I had. I might have learned a few things before the wedding."

"Like what?"

He shrugged as if his button-down shirt had suddenly shrunk. "It might have saved both of us a lot of grief." He tucked a loose strand of hair behind her ear, which sent a shiver of pure delight down her spine. "That's why you should experience as much as you can before you get married."

"You're trying to get me to break my engagement."

"Maybe. But not this way. This is important."

"Why?" Confusion made her mind whirl. Part of her wanted to grasp his tempting offer. Part of her wanted to shove it away, the way he'd set her aside so long ago.

"Because if you don't date for the fun of it, how will you know that you're really marrying the right one?"

"That's insane. Marriage isn't supposed to be fun. Everyone, including you, says it's hard work. Was that all Diane was? A fun date?"

Immediately she regretted that question. "Nick, I'm sorry. I spoke out of turn."

"No." He shook his head. "That's a good point. But there's more to it than that. Maybe we didn't take time to have enough fun. Maybe we didn't date long enough.

"Bottom line, if you don't enjoy your spouse, then it's not worth all the effort." His gaze narrowed. "Life is too hard to go through if you're not with someone who can make you laugh once in a while." He shifted the reins into his other hand. "How does Doug compare to the other men you've dated?"

That stumped her. She rolled her lips inward and studied Calamity's mane. A long moment of silence followed. Billie refused to look at Nick. How could she compare her dream to reality, Nick to Doug? She couldn't lie to Nick. He'd be able to read through her. But she couldn't face the truth, either. She didn't want to see the shock, the slight head shake of pity.

"Why would I want to go out with you? What makes you think we'd have any fun?"

"We did growing up, didn't we?" His jaunty grin made her head whirl.

She pursed her lips. "Yeah, I guess we did. I'm sure it would be an education. Maybe one I should do without. After all, you and Jake taught me some...well, not very sociable manners when I was a kid. Doug might not appreciate anything you have to teach me.''

Nick scowled. ''What did we teach you that was socially unacceptable?''

''The finer points of spitting,'' she said in a matter-of-fact tone, but laughter lurked beneath the surface as she remembered those hot summer afternoons down at Willow's Pond.

''Hey, we taught you not to spit on others. That's socially correct.'' His broad shoulders shook with suppressed laughter. ''You were a natural. You could hit a fly at fifty paces.''

Her mouth twisted with the effort of containing a chuckle. ''You taught me how to box, too. And that got me in trouble when Charlie Wallace and I had a fight on the playground.''

''Only because you bloodied his nose. Otherwise he probably would have been in more trouble for picking on a girl.'' Nick rubbed his jaw. ''You never know, though, that right hook of yours might come in handy. It'll keep me in line. If I get fresh, then I give you permission to wallop me.''

''Yeah, right.'' She rolled her eyes, but her heart hammered in her chest. ''You get fresh with me.''

His smile faded. ''I'm a red-blooded American male. And you're an attractive…beautiful woman. It would be natural—''

''Nick.'' She stepped away from him, uncomfortable with the way his voice made her breath hitch. ''Let's get serious.''

''You've never dated anyone before Doug, have you?'' The warmth and compassion in his voice unbalanced her.

He'd always read her too easily. Irritated, her gaze shot toward him. His eyes darkened to a rich chestnut brown.

She saw only tenderness and sincerity, no pity, no horror. It took the edge off her sharp temper.

"You gave that part of your life up, didn't you?" he asked, glancing at the acres of trees and pasture surrounding them. "That's why you said the Rocking G has been a burden."

A lump lodged in her throat. She'd given up a lot of things to run the ranch. She rubbed her hand along Calamity's shoulder and back. Soon, she'd be able to pursue her own dreams. She'd go to college and become a veterinarian. She'd move forward with her life instead of standing still, marching in place. That's all that mattered anymore.

"You were busy running this blasted ranch, taking the place of your father, then Jake."

"I could handle it. I *can* handle it." Her hackles raised in self-defense. She could feel sorry for herself. But she didn't want or need Nick's pity.

"Of course you can. I didn't mean that. You didn't have much of a choice, did you?"

"Not any more than you did taking over Latham Construction."

His hand cupped her chin, his thumb followed the curve of her jaw and sent sparks along her skin and down her spine. Her heart jolted like a stampede of startled cattle. "Yeah, but it was a part of my dream. Only a piece of it didn't work out for me and my dad. What dreams did you give up, Billie?"

Words, longings and yearnings lodged in her throat. She'd suppressed them for so long, she wasn't sure she could ever express her feelings. She wanted to share her thoughts, her ambitions, all the dreams she'd sacrificed with Nick. But she didn't dare. He might think her a silly schoolgirl all over again. She wanted his respect...or nothing.

After waiting for her to answer, he seemed to sense she wasn't ready. He gave a sigh and grabbed his reins with both hands. "You should have enjoyed a social life like any young woman. And, by God, I'm going to see that you get it. Before you get married and it's too late."

"Nick—"

"I'll handle Doug."

"I don't want you to handle Doug. I don't want a date. I don't want—"

"Sure you do. You want a date with me." He gave her a flirtatious wink that made a denial die on the tip of her tongue.

As he swung himself onto Diablo's back, the saddle creaked with age. She heard the whir of insects around her, a fly buzzing past her ear, a bee settling on a nearby sunflower. Her senses whirred. She felt the devastating effects of Nick roaring back into her life like a twister, stirring up trouble, unsettling her well-thought-out plans.

"I'm going to take you out on the town, Billie. And you're going to have the time of your life."

Again, she felt like the reins of her life had been jerked out of her hands. Yet she was tempted, far too tempted to let Nick take control...this once. But if he did, then she'd be in for the fight of her life, trying to corral her feelings for him all over again.

Chapter Three

What the hell had he gotten himself into? Twenty-four hours later, after he'd appointed himself Billie's "fun date," Nick still questioned his sanity.

Afraid he already knew the answer, knowing it was a purely selfish reason why he'd decided to take Billie out on a date, he realized desire had begun to form deep in his subconscious from the moment he'd set eyes on her in that shimmering wedding gown. Seeing her swathed in white satin that accented her sun-kissed hair and sparkling blue eyes had dredged up feelings he'd never known existed. The changes in her astounded him. And continued to do so each time he looked at her, each time he learned something new about her.

The most troubling question that ran around his brain was, could he stop with one date? Or two? He wasn't sure. And that scared the stuffing out of him.

Nick swerved his Dodge pickup into a parking space at the Angus Café. He'd talked Billie into meeting him for dinner on Saturday night. Of course, he'd invited her fiancé, too. This once. Tension knotted his shoulders. He gritted his teeth and slammed the door shut. Walking toward the steak place, he jammed his hands into his pockets. He'd worked out a plan to present Doug, which would appease any fiancé's suspicions. He hoped it didn't backfire on him.

Steeling his nerve, convincing himself he was doing this for Billie's own good, he opened the door and entered the restaurant. The scent of hickory smoke enticed him to stay. But the sight of Billie nestled against the side of Doug made him want to walk right back out the door. His determination to be sure she'd made the right decision stopped him in his tracks.

Billie looked scrumptious and too damn sexy in an off-the-shoulder dress that wound around her body in provocative waves. The powder blue material enhanced the brighter coloring in her eyes. His gaze followed the long slope of her neck, down to the smooth expanse of golden skin revealed by the wispy dress. Other than in her wedding gown, he'd never seen her dressed this way. Growing up, she'd never worn dresses, never acted like a regular girl fussing over makeup and hair. Seeing her as a woman made him uncomfortable…hot.

Tugging on the unfamiliar tie he'd bought especially for this occasion, Nick walked toward the bar where they stood. He'd guessed right. Doug had dressed as if he was going to the prom. But his suit fit much better than the blue suit Nick had worn to his prom. The urbane businessman hooked a lock of Billie's blond hair behind her ear. The intimate gesture tightened Nick's nerves. Again, he wondered if they'd made love. His hands balled into fists. Irrational anger took hold of him and he stalked toward them.

Using as much willpower as he could muster to keep

from knocking Schaeffer's block off, Nick stuck out his hand, knowing Billie's fiancé would have to release her to shake it. "Hello, Doug."

The man in the dark gray suit gave a broad politician's smile. His grasp was firm, solid, yet nonthreatening. Nick gave a tight squeeze and relished the grimace on Doug's face when his smile faltered. Stepping back, Schaeffer smoothed his hand over his slick black hair.

Nick stepped between the engaged couple, wrapped his arm around Billie and pulled her close to his side. Letting his hand touch her narrow waist, he gave her a hug…brief enough to put more space between her and her fiancé and yet not too long as to cause an immediate threat. But it was long enough to affect him. He breathed in her intriguing jasmine scent. Her warm body molded against him in a natural way before she stiffened. He tuned into everything about her, from the surprise widening her expressive eyes to the way she hesitantly touched his back with her fingertips.

"You look lovely this evening," he said soft enough to be a whisper in her ear but loud enough for her fiancé to hear.

"You clean up nice yourself," she said, her voice breathy.

Doug grabbed her hand, pulling her back to his side. "I picked this dress out. Isn't it something?"

"I'd say the lady makes the outfit." Nick's gaze skimmed down the length of Billie's slight frame, noticing each dip and curve in her figure and the long stretch of her legs. The dress was too short. Too damn revealing. "Without her, it'd be shapeless fabric on a hanger." His gaze shifted back to Doug. "Didn't know you'd studied fashion, Schaeffer."

"It's an important statement in business today. Billie

has to dress for my—our success.'' Doug's gray eyes narrowed on Nick. ''Maybe none of that is important in the construction business. Or do you have more than one pair of work boots?''

Nick bristled at the man's arrogance. Without any reason, other than selfish ones, he decided then and there to stop this wedding. He couldn't let Billie marry Doug Schaeffer. Even if she'd convinced herself she was in love. She deserved better. Unsure of Billie's tender feelings toward her groom-to-be, Nick would tread lightly. He'd show her during their date how she should expect a man to treat her, cherish her. Then, she'd be willing to call off the wedding herself.

''Like with everything else,'' Nick said, his lips thinning into a straight line, ''in the final analysis it's the work that counts. If that doesn't hold up, then neither will the business.'' Maybe that was why Schaeffer Enterprises had been floundering these last couple of years since Doug had taken control of his father's company.

Over the last few hours Nick had done some checking on the diversified company. From oil to real estate, its profits this past year had plummeted. Apparently, Doug had made some poor decisions, sour investments. Doug's interest in Billie stirred Nick's suspicions that something about this engagement wasn't all lovey-dovey. He wondered if Billie was settling for Schaeffer. Was she scared of growing old and being alone? Or was she getting to be as money hungry and fashion conscious as his ex-wife?

He wouldn't stop until he figured out what had brought these two unlikely people together. Then he'd see about getting them apart.

Billie's gaze narrowed on him as if in warning. ''Our

table's ready,'' she said, her voice tight. "Are you men hungry?''

Unable to deny his attraction to her, he recognized the unmistakable heat flowing through his veins. His gaze bore into hers. "More than you'll ever know.''

A healthy pink flushed her cheeks and made his insides glow. "Well, then, let's eat.''

Billie turned on her high heel, wobbled and righted herself before Nick could give her a steadying hand. Uneasy with Nick's hot-as-sin look, she headed toward their table near the back of the restaurant. Prickly sensations rippled along her nerve endings. She sensed Nick's stormy gaze bearing down on her. It made her limbs stiff, and walking in these blasted high heels even more treacherous. Around her waist, Doug's arm settled like a weight. His conceited remark hung around her neck like a yoke. She couldn't complain, though. She'd asked Doug to help her dress more appropriately for business dinners. After all, she wanted to be an asset, not a liability. She wanted him to be proud of her. She only wished he looked at her as Nick had when she'd shown him the Rocking G and all her improvements. Instead, Doug yawned at the mention of cattle or horses. When she wore a new dress, he studied her with a critical eye, noticing every tiny detail and any string or hair out of place. Nick, however, gave her long, appreciative glances that made her senses hum.

Why couldn't Doug make her heart pound, her knees weaken, as Nick once had? As he did now.

That slight confession unnerved her. She was engaged to Doug Schaeffer. For better or worse. Nick Latham had no place in her life anymore. Maybe prewedding jitters were giving her second thoughts. Didn't everyone have them? Wasn't it normal? As much as she tried to convince her mind, her heart contracted with disbelief.

Seated at the table between the men, Billie busied herself with her napkin. The waitress brought the wine list and Nick offered it to Doug. "Since you're my guest, I thought you might like to choose."

"I am quite a connoisseur." Doug opened the wine list with a flourish.

Billie made small talk, keeping to steak preferences and weather predictions, steering clear of politics, religion and business. The succulent odors of garlic and savory herbs filled the dining room, but she'd already lost her appetite. Candlelight cast a soft glow over the men beside her—one arrogantly handsome, the other sexy and scowling with disapproval. Her nerves tightened despite the soft music filtering from the sound system. Howard Cosell would have better suited the mood at their table. He could have given the stats on the two men about to knock heads.

As the waitress took Nick's order, Billie caught herself staring at the simple waves in his brown hair, admiring his ease and confidence, resenting the way he smiled at the busty waitress. Having enjoyed his welcoming hug earlier, she knew the warmth this man could create when he focused his attention on one woman. Whether she liked it or not, she still wanted to be that woman.

Shifting in her seat, she squelched those thoughts. She watched Doug order, heard the commanding tone in his voice as he demanded his steak be cooked "perfectly medium" and saw his quick dismissal of the eager-to-please waitress. What was it about him? He was all any woman could want. Handsome, wealthy, powerful. Still, something she couldn't pinpoint bothered her. Part of her felt as if she'd sold her soul to the devil, just so she could keep her ranch and pursue the life she'd always wanted. What was wrong with taking control of her life? She'd made a decision without the distraction of love and romance. She'd made it logically, practically. She wouldn't back out of it now.

Maybe it was Nick's fault. His presence stirred up doubts, about her impending marriage and herself. Around him, she felt like an awkward teen once again. Resenting his intrusion in her life, she sipped her wine and focused on the dull white tablecloth. Rolling her fork between her fingers, she fidgeted in her chair. But her thoughts stuck to Nick like filings to a magnet.

Her gaze slanted toward him. She noticed the confident tilt of his head, the closeness with which he watched Doug. What was he plotting? Maybe that's why her nerves felt rubbery. What would he say to Doug? On the one hand, she wished Nick would forget his whole scheme to take her out. But on the other, she hoped...

No, she wouldn't do that. Her dreams focused on the future. Not the past. On reality instead of pie-in-the-sky dreams.

When the waitress brought the wine Doug had chosen, her fiancé sniffed the cork, swirled his glass of wine and tasted the wine as if he'd suddenly been appointed king. Billie slanted her gaze toward Nick and noticed his features had tightened.

Over steaks and baked potatoes slathered with butter and cheese, Nick took the first initiative in conversation. "How's business over at Schaeffer Enterprises?"

"Growing." Doug cut into his filet mignon. "We're expanding into new areas. Always looking for new investments."

Anticipating a male-jousting tournament of repeated

jabs for the rest of the night's entertainment, Billie concentrated on her rib eye.

"We've got a new development in the works." Doug patted her thigh beneath the table. She forced herself not to squirm away. "Something that should be quite lucrative."

A frown settled between Nick's brows. He leaned forward, resting his forearms on the table. "And that would be?"

"Can't divulge my secrets yet. Can't be too careful or somebody might beat me to the punch. But it's going to be a sweet deal. Maybe I'll come visit you in a few weeks and discuss business." Doug lifted another bite of steak then paused. "I hear you had a rough start taking over your dad's business."

Nick shrugged. "I wouldn't say that. We might have had a few hurdles to get over after Dad's accident—after he retired, but that was a few years ago. We're on the right track now. It always takes a period of transition when new management takes over."

"Not if it's done right." Doug stuffed a bite into his mouth. He templed his fingers, tapping them against his lips as he chewed. "Things went smoothly at Schaeffer. Of course, if the employees have the same confidence in the incoming president then there shouldn't be a problem."

"Or maybe the old president still has a firm hand in policy," Nick said, his voice cool, his meaning as pointed as a knife blade.

Doug's face reddened.

Billie worried her bottom lip. "How about those Astros?"

Doug ignored her suggestion to change the subject to baseball and stabbed another piece of meat. He chomped down on it and swallowed hard, his gaze pinpointing Nick. "So, you're finally turning a profit, Latham?"

"Always have."

Billie's gaze volleyed like a Ping-Pong ball between the two men, her nerves stretching with each shot.

"Do you only handle old accounts, ones that your dad generated, or do you consider new opportunities?" Doug sipped his wine with a flourish, as if he'd scored a fatal serve.

Nick gave a tolerant smile. He looked calm and unruffled, like a prizefighter toying with an easy opponent. "Latham Construction is always interested in new business. We're expanding into development. We're looking for solid offers, though, no risky gambles."

"Don't take chances, huh?" Doug sneered and tapped the linen napkin against both corners of his mouth.

"Every day," Nick said. "Just not interested in a losing proposition."

Irritated at their male egos, Billie cleared her throat. "Nick—" she gave him a warning look "—tell us what sites you're working on now."

"Sure, tell us what road you're hoeing." Doug yawned, sliding his arm along the back of Billie's chair. He gave her shoulder a squeeze.

This time, she leaned forward, pretending to put more effort in eating her potato. Her movement only brought her closer to Nick. She noticed his white collar rubbing against his tanned neck, his dark hair curling along his nape, his spicy cologne that made her insides tremble. Being near him always seemed to get her in trouble. She'd be better off if she kept her focus on her fiancé...or her future. But Nick seeped into her thoughts, just as he'd slipped into her dreams last night.

"It might be too complicated for Schaeffer to compre-

hend," Nick said, taking another verbal jab at Doug.
"But I've got seven contracts in the works at the moment. Another starting in July and another in August."

"Aren't you spreading yourself a little thin?" Doug's
voice sounded tight.

"Not at all. But we're running at full capacity." Nick
focused on his steak before giving Doug a pointed stare.
"So about this new project. When will you be able to
discuss it? When you get the money?"

"We have the backing," Doug said. "Money isn't an
issue."

"What is?" Nick asked.

"Timing." Doug sipped his merlot. "We might just
need a few construction crews. Would your company be
up to the task?"

"What do you need? More roads in Bonnet?" Nick
asked, humor lacing his words. "Or are you expecting
Houston traffic to back up this far?"

"No, of course not. But we'll need some roads widened. And a few side streets paved in the development."

"Where's it going to be?"

Curious, Billie glanced at her fiancé. He hadn't mentioned a new project to her. Of course, they rarely spoke
of business, except for contacts he needed to make and
how a pretty woman by his side could help him achieve
more.

"You're really interested in this, aren't you?" Doug
dabbed his mouth with the linen napkin. He tossed it
beside his plate. "Look, I tell you what. Since I'm on
the city council, I could suggest your company for the
job. My opinion's highly respected. If I give the nod, then
the others will agree. I like to help out old friends in
need."

The lines in Nick's face hardened like cement. His

gaze bore into Doug with an intensity that made a shiver run through Billie. She groaned inwardly.

"My company's not a charity case." Firm conviction rang in Nick's voice. "We'd be happy to put in a bid. But we *don't* want favors."

"Sure." Doug winked. "I understand."

Heat emanated from Nick. Billie saw the tick in his jaw and knew he'd about reached the end of his rope. A headache inched around her skull. "Why don't we discuss something other than business?"

The two men stared at each other as if a battle line had been drawn. The ropelike cords in Nick's neck stood out under his taut skin. Slowly, Doug shifted his gaze to Billie. "We boring you, babe?"

She bristled. "Not at all. I own and operate my own business."

"Not quite the same as the business world." Doug laughed. "Of course, I've run into a few associates who are bullheaded. I wouldn't have minded using a cattle prod on them a time or two." He shifted in his chair and gave her a condescending look that made her want to put him through a cattle chute. "Go on and tell us your latest plans for the wedding. What flowers have you picked? What colors for the bridesmaids?"

A grin split Nick's chiseled features. He leaned back, crossing his arms over his chest. "Yeah, Billie, tell us all about your plans."

She realized she'd made a mistake changing the subject. She didn't have to protect Nick. He could take care of himself. She forked her potato, drawing furrows with the tines through the white fluff. "Well, my dress is almost finished."

"And it looks incredible on you," Nick said.

"You saw it?" The corners of Doug's mouth pulled down. "When?"

"Yesterday." Billie's voice squeaked. Her head pounded. She felt like a juicy bone being circled by two snarling canines.

"I was over at the ranch," Nick explained. "I hadn't seen Martha in a while. She's like a mother to me. Billie was in the middle of her fitting. So, I got a sneak preview." He lifted his wineglass in salute. "You're a lucky man, Schaeffer."

Doug's gaze flicked back and forth between Billie and Nick as if unsure whether he should be jealous or proud. Without another word, he signaled the waitress for dessert.

Unsure of her fiancé's conclusions, Billie wanted to reassure him...as much as herself. There was nothing between her and Nick. Nothing at all. And there never would be.

She edged her chair closer to Doug's. "Do you know what Mother suggested yesterday?"

He gave a slight shrug of disinterest.

She figured Doug would find out sooner or later, probably sooner with Nick grinning from ear to ear. She might as well deliver the bomb as delicately as possible. She laughed, trying to ease into it and make a joke out of the situation. "That Nick walk me down the aisle and give me away!"

But Doug didn't find any humor. Billie's nerves stretched to the breaking point as wedges of creamy cheesecake and cups of coffee were served. Doug sat back, his expression mild, almost blank. Nick's mouth twisted in a smug I-won-that-round grin.

"Why would she suggest such a stupid thing?" Doug asked, his tone flat.

Immediately her spine stiffened. "Nick's always been like family, kind of like another big brother to me."

"Thought we'd outgrown all those adolescent years," Doug said.

"Some of us have," Nick answered. "But some bonds can never be broken or forgotten. Martha Gunther took me under her wing when my mom died. Dad was always traveling and working. Back then, he'd go anywhere for a construction job. And often I stayed with Jake and Billie."

"One big, happy family, huh?" Doug asked, his frown showing his doubt. "But you haven't been around much in the last few years."

"Family is always family," Billie added. "Time and distance can't change that." She knew Nick's absence had been her fault. She caught the gleam in her "big brother's" eye and decided to put him in his place. "He tortured me almost as much as Jake. Made my life miserable…like a good big brother should."

"And I'm not done yet." Nick grinned. "We had some good times, Jake and I. Tormenting a little sister can be a full-time task. I've fallen down on my duty lately. But I'll make up for lost time."

She gave him a teasing punch in his bicep but added more zest than she should have. His arm felt rock hard, and she rubbed her knuckles under the table. She eyed him warily then turned a sweet smile on Doug, who frowned at his coffee.

"You name it, they did it." She chuckled, giving in to the fond memories. Laughter had once filled their house with love and acceptance. What had happened to the easy smiles? Hard work and responsibility had replaced the humor. Jake had died. Nick had left for greener pastures. Loneliness had replaced the fun.

An edge of her heart opened back up to Nick. He and his many practical jokes had made life in the Gunther household fun and exciting. She missed that. She realized then, she'd missed Nick. Missed the closeness. Missed the familiarity, the special bond.

His eyes twinkled with merriment. "Jake used to tackle Billie the Kid. Together, we'd hold her down and tickle her."

"God, my sides hurt just remembering." Billie hugged her middle.

He laughed. "You'd scream and holler until your dad would come to your rescue. Remember? You were sure a daddy's girl."

"I think Dad just got tired of the noise and—"

"I hate to interrupt this little family reunion," Doug said, his voice tight. "But who's going to pay the check?" He nodded toward the leather folder the waitress had laid on the table. "It's getting late."

Nick reached for it. "My pleasure. Since I invited you two for dinner." Slipping his credit card between the covers, he cut his eyes toward Billie. "What kind of a prank could I pull at your wedding? I've got to do something for old times' sake."

Her heart sank at the thought of her wedding and Nick there only as a practical jokester and her escort down the aisle.

Candlelight caught a glimmer of mischief in his hazel depths. Even though he stood over six feet tall, he looked like a little boy, bright-eyed with excitement. It was that little boy she'd fallen in love with. And she figured part of her still loved him.

But only as a friend.

"Don't most older brothers pull a prank or two before

the little sister goes off on her honeymoon?'' he asked. ''You won't take offense will you, Schaeffer?''

''Not at all. Good luck, though. Nobody knows where we're going,'' the unruffled bridegroom said. ''I had to be cautious about making reservations. Too many fraternity brothers would love to get me back after the stunts I've pulled.''

Billie's brow arched, surprised by her fiancé's revelation. She hadn't thought of Doug as a prankster. He rarely laughed around her. He never seemed to relax, either. They'd never really discussed their honeymoon. Frankly, Billie had wanted to avoid the delicate topic. All she wanted to do was enroll for her fall classes. But Doug had insisted they do something special. He'd promised to take care of everything. And she'd tried to put it out of her mind.

''Good thinking,'' Nick said with a nod. ''Never can be too careful. You might make two separate reservations under different names. Maybe even separate flights.'' He leaned back, tipping his chair on its back legs. ''I've been trying to think of a perfect gift for you two. I may have just figured it out.''

Doug leaned forward. Billie eyed Nick, wary of the tricks up his sleeves.

''It occurred to me, Billie, that you might need to do a little shopping in Houston since Bonnet doesn't have many shops. I don't know what you'll need, but you could look for your groom's gift—'' he gave Doug a wink ''—maybe even some sexy lingerie for the honeymoon.''

''I like that idea, babe.''

Billie suppressed a shiver. ''I'm sure I can find everything I need right here in town.''

''I doubt that,'' Doug said. ''You deserve better than

this town can offer. There's probably last-minute things you need for the wedding, too. Remember, we're inviting important business associates. Every tiny detail of the wedding is crucial.''

"Houston has the 'in' stores,'' Nick added.

"I'm on a budget, guys,'' she said, irritation seeping into her voice.

"But this would be my treat. I'd foot the bill.'' He shot a glance at Doug. "My pleasure.''

"That's not necessary, Nick. Doug can take me to Houston.'' She turned to her fiancé, suddenly not at all sure she wanted to go off to the big city with her "big brother.'' She felt like Little Red Riding Hood sitting on the edge of her grandmother's bed and noticing shiny, pointed fangs.

Nick snorted. "Ah, Schaeffer's probably too busy with his company for a shopping spree.''

"I am swamped, babe. And we're already taking a week for our honeymoon.'' He gave her thigh another irritating squeeze.

Billie frowned.

"Of course, you could stay with me,'' Nick suggested. "I'm not home much, but I can show you around some.'' He gave her a wink that elevated her blood pressure. "You could borrow my extra car, and I'll point you toward the Galleria.''

"Good idea.'' Doug nodded. "Take a week or so, babe. Enjoy yourself. I'll give you a list of stores where you might find some nice clothes. Some of that sexy lingerie Nick mentioned.''

Irritated at Doug's interest in her lingerie and Nick's suggestion, she put up another argument. "Who'll take care of the ranch?''

"I'll handle everything," Doug said. "Don't worry your pretty li'l head about anything."

She jerked her arm away from his condescending pat. "My cattle. My worry."

"Hire someone," Nick suggested, "to run things while you're gone."

She and Doug had discussed just that possibility for when she began her college courses in the fall, but she hadn't found anybody she trusted yet. "It's not that easy to find someone capable and responsible."

"Sure it is," Doug added. "What's it take to toss a bucket of feed into a trough? Certainly not a Harvard IQ."

"It takes more than that," Nick said. "I remember all the work we did as kids."

"See—" Doug snapped his fingers "—a kid could do it!"

Biting her tongue, Billie decided at that moment she wanted Doug to learn how much was involved in running the Rocking G. Maybe then she'd earn his respect. More than that, a trip to Houston in Nick's company would prove once and for all that she was over him. That he no longer had a hold on her heart.

"Good," she said with a confident smile. "You handle the ranch, Doug." She turned a sweet smile on Nick. "So, big brother, when do you want me?"

His smoldering glance made her doubt the wisdom of her words. Fact was, she wanted Nick. She always had. And going to Houston was about as wise as standing under a tree during a thunderstorm.

Chapter Four

Don't worry your pretty li'l head about anything.

Billie remembered Doug's words two days later as she climbed out of Nick's truck and stepped into a whole new world. Worry? What was there to worry about? She'd turned her ranch over to a gum-popping, pimple-faced eighteen-year-old. She had a zillion wedding plans to coordinate. She was frazzled, all right, and not just about the cattle and what kind of flowers to order for her bouquet.

Yesterday she'd tried to show Doug every aspect of the ranch and written copious notes about the horses' feed along with other essential information. With her heart in her throat, she'd agreed to hire Harold Jacobson's youngest son to handle things. If the teenager needed any help, he could always call on his father. Mr. Jacobson had always offered Billie advice and a helping hand with the Rocking G. While she was gone, Doug would oversee the teenager's work. This morning she'd turned her back on everything she'd worked so hard to build, kissed her mother goodbye and headed to Houston with Nick. So what was she so worried about?

Nick. That's what. What had she agreed to?

Here she was, with Nick, alone. It should have been the most natural thing in the world. They were like brother and sister. But then again, they weren't. Was that why her heart beat ten times faster than normal? Was that the reason she'd entertained dreams about him last night? Was that why she kept glancing in his direction, noticing the coarse blond hairs along his forearms, the calluses on his hands, the way his eyes turned like autumn leaves to amber when he looked at her?

As a teenager she'd pictured herself running off with him so many times that now it felt a little too familiar. But at the same time, it seemed completely different from her naive imaginings. Her fantasies had always been filled with romantic delusions and usually ended with a wedding and Nick sealing their vows with a kiss.

Well, she was planning a wedding all right, but not with Nick. He'd never thought of her as anything more than a li'l sister. Maybe that's how it was supposed to be. But somehow it made her feel empty inside, like she was missing something. But what?

Why did everyone make such a big deal out of love and romance? Her way was much better. No jittery nerves. No uneasy stomach. No delusions.

She had a wealthy fiancé. Her Cinderella wedding was around the corner. Soon she'd pursue the life she'd always wanted. But it was missing a vital element—Nick.

The realization made her want to weep. Squaring her shoulders, reminding herself that she *never* cried, she determined she was better off on her practical path.

She glanced toward Nick. Like any country boy, he had a gun rack along the cab of his truck. Instead of shotguns, though, it held rolled-up blueprints. The contrast made her smile and helped her begin to sense the changes in him.

He alighted from the truck, looking at ease, his gold-tinged brown hair ruffled by the wind, his chambray shirt starched and creased, emphasizing his straight shoulders, compact chest and rippling muscles. Handsome and sexy as any Hollywood heartthrob, no wonder she'd had a crush on him as a kid. But she wasn't the same naive Billie the Kid. She knew better than to give away her heart.

Still, the steady beat accelerated. Blood raced through her veins at nerve-tingling speed. Nerves, she thought. She felt like the country mouse visiting the big city. That's all it was—nerves.

Which struck her as odd. She almost expected herself to feel uncomfortable with her fiancé. After all, they were different; they ran in different circles, they'd never been friends. Doug sipped brandy with clients while she drank beer after a hard day working cattle.

But Nick! He'd been like her. Once. But not anymore.

Maybe it was good for her to come here, to see the changes, that she and Nick were separated by more than time and distance. She hadn't expected to feel this raw, aching disappointment, though. This is what she'd come here to prove—that her little-girl fantasies of Nick no longer made her heart pound.

But he did.

She glanced around at his "home," feeling like Dorothy landing in Oz. The two-story brick monstrosity rivaled Doug's family mansion in size. Surprised by her childhood playmate's obvious wealth, she stood outside his three-car garage, behind his shiny black Jaguar. "This is your second car?"

"Yeah." He slammed his truck door shut. "It's not too reliable."

She shook her head. On the Rocking G, if equipment didn't work, it was replaced by something practical, sensible, dependable. Luxuries were a rarity. She'd expected Nick's second car to be a sedate four-door sedan or a junky pickup. What should she expect from Nick now that they were both older? He was a stranger to her. Where was the boy she'd grown up with? Where was the Nick she knew so well, who'd worn patched-up jeans and laughed at the Doug Schaeffers who flaunted their expensive toys?

"So why keep it?" she asked.

He shrugged. "It's a keepsake, a reminder..."

Of his ex-wife? "Of?"

His sudden frown deepened, and she realized she'd jabbed a sensitive subject. "Old times."

Feeling as if a cold, wet washcloth had been placed over her heart, Billie sensed a sorrow in Nick and a brick wall rise between them as thick and tall as the walls of his house. She'd hoped he'd moved beyond his divorce. For his sake, of course, not for any other personal reason, she reminded herself. But maybe he hadn't. Maybe he still loved his ex-wife, Diane. That thought gave a sharp stab right in the center of Billie's heart.

"Come on in," he said, lifting her suitcase out of the bed of the truck and carrying it to the back door. After unlocking the dead bolt and disengaging the alarm system, he ushered her inside and around a corner where she stopped dead in her tracks.

She felt her jaw go slack and managed to close her mouth from gaping. The kitchen looked like it belonged in her mother's *Southern Living* magazine. Sunlight slanted through a bank of windows along the back of the house, making the wood floors and matching cabinets gleam with polish. She detected the lingering scent of pine cleaner in the room. Beyond the covered porch, she could see a sparkling blue pool surrounded by flowering bougainvillea and bright red hibiscus. This wasn't a home, this was a showplace.

Nick tromped through the kitchen, his boot heels clomping against the floor in a careless manner. Billie felt like she ought to take her boots off and tiptoe her way through the house. All she could think was, who cleaned this place? Who scrubbed the counters, mopped the floors and made the paned windows sparkle like diamonds?

"Are you coming?" Nick asked, pausing to look back over his shoulder at her.

She stood on a thin narrow rug and glanced down at her scuffed boots. "Shouldn't I take these off first?"

"This isn't Japan," he said. "Come on in. Relax. Make yourself at home."

"But...what about...what if I scuff up your floors?" How many times had she been lectured at home for doing just that?

"Don't worry about it. We'll dump some sawdust on them later and do a little boot-scootin' if you want." He gave her a wink that soothed her worries and turned her stomach inside out all at the same time. Relief flooded her. This was Nick, her friend, her big brother. Maybe he hadn't changed so much. Maybe she hadn't, either. Which didn't settle her nerves at all. Because maybe he still had a firm hold on her heart.

"Your room's upstairs," he said.

"Where's yours?" she asked automatically, suddenly very much aware that they'd be sleeping in the same house. Although in this place, it might seem like different continents.

"It's on the first floor." His grin widened. "Don't worry, you're safe here with me."

The quick reminder that he wasn't interested in her— had never been interested in her—tripped up her confidence. Maybe she shouldn't be worried about Nick so much as her simmering reactions to him! She had to get him out of her mind and heart. And fast!

Irritated at the thoughts spinning around her head and more determined than ever to feel nothing for Nick, she followed him through the oversize family room with ceilings that seemed tall enough to comfortably house a herd of giraffes. The hunter green and burgundy decor made a blurry impression on her, but she noticed the supple leather furniture, the expensive artwork along the paneled walls, the glazed pottery and cut-glass adorning shelves and filling curio cabinets. In her head, she heard her momma saying, "Don't touch, Billie! Be careful not to break anything."

He'd told her to relax. How could she, fearing she might break something at the slightest wrong turn? How could she relax when she couldn't seem to take her mind off Nick and the foreign world in which he now resided?

By the time she reached the wide, swooping staircase, he'd already reached the top. She placed a tentative hand on the gleaming wood banister and started the climb, noticing the arched windows along the front of the house, the sprawling dining room table below her and the shimmering chandelier in the entryway. She stepped onto the landing and realized she'd lost her guide.

"Nick?"

"This way," he called from somewhere to her left.

Winding her way through a long hallway, she found

him in a delicate blue and lace bedroom. He'd already laid her suitcase on the window seat near the four-poster canopy bed. The scent of lilacs floated on the air and made the room even more feminine. She glanced down at her worn boots and faded jeans. Embarrassment stung her cheeks. She didn't belong here, in Nick's house. Or in his life.

Too aware of the quiet descending on them, she managed to say, "You have a beautiful house, er..." Was that the right word to describe this place? It seemed lacking somehow. "Er...home."

Nick shrugged. "It was my ex-wife's project."

That explained a lot. No wonder it didn't reflect Nick, the man she thought she knew. Suddenly curious about why a woman would decorate a place to her liking then abandon it, she asked, "You kept it after the divorce?"

"Yeah, she had other projects by then."

"I see." But she didn't. Why hadn't he sold it? Was he hanging on to the past as she was grabbing for a future? "What'd Diane get? The dog? The yacht?" she asked, then wished she hadn't. "Sorry, Nick." She ducked her head and rubbed her palms along her jeans, feeling like a clod just in from the fields. "It's none of my business."

He laughed. The vibrating sound warmed her. "Don't ever be sorry about asking me anything." He rubbed his hand along his jaw thoughtfully, erasing his quick-flash smile. "We didn't have a yacht. If we had, Diane probably would have taken it. She got what she wanted— more money. And a more suitable husband."

Billie blinked, surprised by his statement as well as the resentment clipping his words. "She's already remarried?"

He nodded. "Married a doctor of some kind." He met

her gaze squarely then. "But she didn't get the dog. He's mine." His mouth curled enticingly. "I'll pick him up from Jody later today."

"Jody?" she asked, a sudden surge of jealousy stealing over her like a cool wintery breeze.

"My foreman. Sometimes I think he knows the business better than I do. Anyway, he takes care of Buddy when I'm out of town."

"Buddy's your dog?"

"You'll like him."

Knowing beyond a shadow of a doubt that she would, she made a slow circle in place, looking at the white molding along the top of the pale blue walls, then out the windows, down at the golf-course-sanctioned lawn. "Do you ever get lost in this place?"

Nick laughed. "Not anymore. I'll give you a map later."

She gave him a tight smile, not sure if he was joking. She might need a diagram or she could leave a few bread crumbs along the way to find her way back. Maybe her heart would lead her home. Because she couldn't stay in Nick's world. She'd planned her own future, and he wasn't a part of it.

"If you don't mind," Nick said, "why don't you get settled while I go check a couple of construction sites and call in to the office."

"Do you need any help?" she asked, wondering what she'd do here all alone without chores or some minor mishap needing her attention.

"I can handle it," he said. "I won't be long, maybe a couple of hours. I'll leave the keys to the Jag on the kitchen table."

She nodded and sank onto the thick comforter after Nick left the room. For some strange reason her legs felt about as reliable as a newborn calf's. Her skin tingled. Her mind felt numb. Was she overworked? Had she pushed herself for too long? Or was she still unable to believe she was sitting in Nick Latham's house—still wanting to be a part of his life, a part of his heart, but knowing that was an impossibility.

Feeling the heart-wrenching impact of that thought, she pushed herself to her feet and gave herself a grand tour of the house. With each room, she was reminded of the differences in their lives. She got lost only once but found her way out of a maze of hallways, back downstairs and into the kitchen. After a stroll around the pool and over the immaculate grounds, she made herself a peanut butter and jelly sandwich. Before she'd swallowed the last bite, the garage door opened. A golden retriever, tail wagging, fur flouncing and tongue lolling, bounded into the house, announcing his master's arrival.

"Hey, Buddy," she said, standing to greet the gentle giant with a friendly rub and scratch behind the ears. The dog gave her a slobbery kiss along the cheek. She heard a rusty chuckle and glanced up at Nick walking in the door.

"I see you two have met."

"Instant friends," she replied, running her fingers through Buddy's thick, luxuriant coat.

"You always were good with animals."

A faint blush warmed her cheeks. "Anybody could make friends with Buddy."

"Not that pesky squirrel out back. Or the gray Siamese up the street." Nick walked across the room, grabbed Buddy's collar and hauled him off Billie. "Or Diane."

"Buddy and your wife—ex-wife—didn't get along?"

He shrugged. "That's not too surprising. We didn't,

either.'' The side of his mouth stretched into a wry grin. ''Guess it worked out for the best. Right, Buddy?''

The dog panted and offered a resounding bark that rang in Billie's ears. She laughed and rubbed the fuzzy head. The dog's soft brown eyes stared up at her with interest. ''How'd you get a silly name like Buddy, huh?''

''Short for Budweiser,'' Nick answered. ''That's one reason Diane didn't like him.''

''Because of his name?''

He nodded. ''She wanted to name him Shakespeare or Lancelot.'' He gave a sneer. ''But it was my dog, and I chose Budweiser. And she resented that…and a few other things.''

''Like?'' she asked before catching her mistake. When would she learn to quit being so nosy about Nick?

''Like how much a big dog like this sheds,'' he said before she could apologize again. ''How Buddy likes to sleep in my bed. How he likes to drink water out of the toilet.''

Billie laughed. ''So she didn't like waking up to a cold, wet nose, huh?'' She imagined the sleek, sophisticated Diane being pushed off the bed by an oversize canine. ''You only need a couple of weeks to fix bad habits like that.''

''But *I* wasn't willing to learn.'' He winked.

''Oh, gotcha!'' Billie popped the last bite of her sandwich into Buddy's mouth and received a lip-chomping smack for her efforts. The dog gazed up at her, his tail dusting the floor behind him in an arc. ''I don't have any more food.''

''Once you feed him, he's your shadow forever,'' Nick said, grabbing the dog's collar. ''There's only one thing that'll get his mind off food.''

"What's that?" she asked, wondering what would finally get her mind off Nick.

"A game of chase," he said, moving toward the back door.

A minute later they were running around the backyard, chasing the dog, acting like two little kids. They ran the dog in circles, jumped over bushes, skimmed the edge of the pool. Buddy barked and dodged them. Nick and Billie laughed until their sides pinched. It felt like old times, fun, frolicking, playful times when they hadn't had a care in the world, when they'd been friends, comrades, pals.

But times changed, just as people did. Finally, panting, Buddy plopped down in the cool shade of a live oak tree, his pink tongue hanging out of his mouth. Nick bent over, propping his hands on his knees, his sides heaving. Billie sank down onto a pool lounge chair and tipped her face toward the clear blue sky and drew in a deep breath.

After a few minutes of comfortable silence she said, "Thanks for inviting me here, Nick."

He looked at her, his gaze solemn, penetrating. "You're welcome."

She leaned back against the strips of plastic and stretched her legs out. Placing her hands behind her head, she said, "I feel totally decadent."

"How come?"

"I should be hauling hay, mending a fence or something useful. Instead I'm just lazing around."

"I've got a lightbulb needs changing in the utility room," he offered.

"I'll do it."

"That was a joke," he said. "Enjoy this like you would a vacation."

"What's that?" she asked, closing her eyes and absorbing the heat from the noon-high sun.

He laughed with her. The easiness between them stretched into another lengthy silence. Billie kept her eyes shut and listened to the dog's heavy breathing, an insect buzzing by her ear. She concentrated on relaxing each muscle in her body. All she needed now was some cute waiter to come offer her a chilled margarita or Nick to give her a back rub. No, no, no. That kind of thinking would get her into trouble.

"You should get plenty of rest on your honeymoon." Nick's whiskey-smooth voice wasted her efforts as she suddenly tensed.

She'd avoided thinking about her honeymoon with Doug, ignored the way it made her feel restless, uneasy. Most brides probably felt that way, she figured. Sloughing aside those disturbing thoughts, she decided to keep right on ignoring the fact that the wedding and her honeymoon were fast approaching.

"Billie?" Nick's voice sounded close, too close, as if his breath could tickle her ear.

She jerked open her eyes. He lounged in the chair beside hers, his face turned toward her, his gaze hotter than the sun and making her insides squirm.

"Hmm?" she mumbled, trying to sound nonchalant.

"Are you missing Doug?" His tone deepened.

Was that a sneer she detected curling his lip? "Why should I?"

"If you're in love," he offered, the skin between his brows bunching into a frown, "it'd be natural."

She sighed and settled back into her relaxed mode. "Nick, we only left this morning," she countered. "I haven't had a chance to miss him yet." Then a thought struck her. How was the Jacobson boy handling the ranch? Was everything okay? Had Doug remembered to tell the teenager to feed those heifers in the back pasture? "I need to call and check on the ranch."

She started to rise, but Nick caught her arm. He was closer than she'd thought. She stared into his churning amber eyes, noting the mixture of concern and suspicion darkening them. Frozen by his warm hand on her arm, holding her in place, she felt her pulse skitter, her breath catch in her throat.

"Wait," he said. The urgency in his tone set her nerves on edge. "Billie." His voice caressed her name in a way no one else could. "Do you love Doug?"

Chilled by his pointed question, she frowned. "Telling you yes wouldn't stop your scheme to have this wedding called off. So what's the point of agreeing or not?"

"I have to know."

"Why?" She lifted her chin in a challenge.

"Because I don't think you're happy."

"Marriage doesn't make someone happy, Nick. You should know that."

Not denying it, he met her gaze squarely, not backing away, not releasing her, either. "Too damn well. That's why I know how important this is." She shifted uncomfortably beneath his intense stare, tried to pull her arm away from him, but his hand tightened around her wrist, his fingers easily circling the fine bones. "What would make you happy, Billie the Kid?"

Her heart contracted like a fist closing around it. When was the last time someone had asked her what she wanted...needed...craved? Her longings jammed in her throat like traffic on the freeway. But when would Nick see her as more than a kid? "For you to stop calling me that nickname."

A flicker in his eyes made her regret her harsh words.

''Done. But I'm sure that's not your heart's desire. What is?''

''Nick—''

''Tell me, Billie.''

She twisted her arm out of his grasp and stood, moving away from him and the powerful effect he had on her. Her back to him, she squared her shoulders and stiffened her spine against the weakness he caused in her. ''What makes you think I'm not happy?''

''With Schaeffer?'' He laughed, a caustic sound that chilled her blood in spite of the warm day. ''Because he *can't* make you happy.''

''How would you know?''

''I know.'' A tender, seductive tone stole into his voice and made her skin tighten with anticipation.

Fighting the urge within her to see if *he* could make her happy, she whirled around, turning on him. ''Yeah? What do you think would make me happy? Money? A fancy house? You?'' She laughed but felt bitterness rise inside her and unshed tears burn the backs of her eyes. ''I don't think so. Maybe I was foolish once to think such a crazy notion. But I've wised up. Don't worry about me, Nick. I know exactly what I'm doing.''

''Do you?'' He crossed his arms over his chest and settled back in his chair. ''I'm not so sure.''

She glared down at him, not knowing what to say to end this inappropriate conversation. This is why she hadn't wanted to come to Houston with Nick. She knew he would try to change her mind. He'd try to confuse her and, in her hesitation, get her to call off the wedding. All because *he* didn't approve of *her* groom. She'd thought he'd at least have waited longer than a couple of hours before putting her on the defensive.

"You don't have to be the one that's sure. I do. And I am."

"You're wrong. If I'm going to give the bride away, then I've got to be damn sure you're not walking blindfolded into a disaster."

"Then don't give me away. I'd rather walk the aisle alone."

"I'm sure you would, but I already agreed."

"Mother will understand."

"No, she won't. Do you want to explain it to her? Do you want to tell her the real reason why you don't want me to walk you down the aisle?"

Her heart stopped. Did he know? Did he know she still fought those deep feelings for him?

"I already told her the reason. And you were there."

His look told her he didn't believe her, not totally. But she didn't worry about convincing him as much as she worried about convincing herself that her feelings for him had died a long time ago. Their gazes met, locked, challenged each other like old times.

"Schaeffer doesn't love you," he stated, his voice soft as a whispered kiss.

Feeling the impact of it like a heavy blow, she flinched. Her world tilted off center for a moment and she struggled to right it. "He told you this?"

"Didn't have to," he declared, unfolding his arms to grip the sides of his lounge chair. "I could tell."

Her confidence crumpled like a paper sack. Was she so unlovable that he didn't believe a man could fall in love with her? She remembered how the story of her impending marriage spread like wildfire through Bonnet. The older folks speculated on why Doug Schaeffer had chosen Billie the Kid Gunther, the tomboy of Liberty County, as his bride. Nick's doubt hurt even more, like a knife carving a piece out of her heart, a piece she thought had been removed when she'd been rejected by him. The throbbing pain resonated through her body. But she couldn't let him see how his words hurt her. She couldn't let him see. She wouldn't give in to the heartache. Not now. Not this time.

"I thought you got a degree in engineering, not psychology," she said, tightening her restraint over her emotions.

"A man in love doesn't try to change his fiancée. A man in love bends over backward trying to please the woman he intends to marry. He'll—"

"Are you talking about yourself, Nick, or Doug?" She placed her hands on her hips. "Didn't you say you weren't willing to learn a few easy lessons to make your bride happy with Buddy? Weren't you in love with Diane?"

"Not by then. But I was at first. I was when we got married." The lines surrounding his mouth deepened.

"What happened?" she asked, too curious for her own good and glad for a change of focus in the conversation. Her heart pounded in her chest as she waited to hear if Nick's heartache matched her own.

A hard glint entered his eyes and his expression closed like a gate shutting to keep out trespassers. "It doesn't matter now."

"I think it does," she said. "You want to know if I'm prepared to commit to Doug till death do us part. Maybe I can learn from your mistakes."

He shook his head. "My relationship with Diane has nothing to do with you and Doug."

"You still think of me as a kid sister, don't you?" she accused, feeling her blood boiling with frustration and resentment. "That's it, isn't it? You just simply don't think I'm mature enough to make a decision the magnitude of marriage. Well, I've got news for you, Nick, I've grown up a lot since you left Bonnet. I had to.''

"I know, Billie. I don't think you're a child. But you are naive, sheltered. That's why I wanted you to get out some, to date for the fun of it. To experience a little more of life.''

"If you think running a ranch on my own, and all that entails, is leading a sheltered life, then you ought to try it for a week.'' She shook her head. "That date idea was just an excuse to get me away from Doug, so you could convince me I shouldn't get married. You don't know anything about me. You don't know that I—'' She stopped herself from elaborating. She didn't want his sympathy. She wanted him to leave her alone.

"What?'' he prompted, pushing himself up out of the chair to stand in front of her.

"That's the difference between you and Doug. He sees me as an adult. A woman who knows her own mind. He treats me as an equal. You still treat me like a child.''

His gaze burned bright, a fiery hunger consuming her. That penetrating look sapped the strength right out of her knees. Right then, in broad daylight, he hauled her against him. Her breath left her body in a whoosh.

There was one brief second when understanding clicked in her brain. He was going to kiss her. Nick was going to kiss her! She could have no more pushed him away than she could draw another breath. His gaze shifted toward her mouth before he took it, kissing her like a man should kiss a woman, giving as much as he took. Underlying the forceful pressure he used, his hands gentled, his mouth became tender. Her heart melted. Something inside her burst. Heat radiated through her limbs. She kissed him back, demanding from him more than he could ever return. She knew then, with her arms wrapped around his neck, that Nick still owned her heart. Every shattered piece of it.

Bad decision. Bad. Bad. Bad.

Nick held Billie against his chest, feeling her soft curves mold against him. His hands bracketed her arms. His mouth claimed hers. And he didn't want to let her go. Even though he knew he should. He knew the kiss was a mistake.

With each second her fiery heat wrapped around his heart. She tasted hot as a chili pepper, her strength like fire in his blood. Yet there was a sweetness, a tender need, that he felt in her velvety soft lips. She fit against him, as if she'd been made for him, her lithe body meeting his squarely. He drank in the taste and smell of her as though he'd lived in the desert far too long. Maybe he had. Maybe he needed this. Maybe Billie did, too.

His body thrummed with the knowledge that she didn't love Doug. He knew it with solid conviction. It filled him with hope, relief, then confusion. Why would she want to marry Schaeffer? Why would she throw her life away?

And why the hell was he still kissing her? Hadn't he proven his point? Hadn't he shown her he thought of her not as a child but as a desirable woman?

Overwhelmed by his response, surprised by her eagerness, he jerked his mouth away from hers. His labored breathing sounded harsh in his own ears. Confused as if he'd walked into a dense fog, he braced himself for her reaction—a slap, a curse word....

But she looked up at him, her gaze soft like a hazy sky, her lips parted, moist, too damn soft, and her skin flushed as if they'd just made love. Dammit! She looked like a woman who wanted more.

But he had nothing to give her. He had to stop anything else from happening now or in the future. He might not want her marrying Doug Schaeffer, but he wasn't volunteering to stand in as her groom.

"See?" he said, his voice booming like a jackhammer, breaking the fragile silence between them, his confidence returning. "I knew you didn't love Doug."

"What?" she asked blinking, pushing away from him. Her hands on his shoulders balled into fists.

"That was a test," he stated, deciding it must have been an unconscious one. "Any engaged woman who can kiss a man other than her fiancé like that is *not* ready for marriage."

"Why you conceited, arrogant—" She crossed her arms over her chest and glared at him, her eyes like lasers. "You think you're so smart, don't you?"

"I managed to get past all the bull you were feeding me."

She shook her head. "Kissing you was just some harmless fun, you imbecile. Just like you told me I should have."

That took the steam right out of his engine. She didn't need to have any more fun. Neither did he. But then he knew he was in deeper trouble than he realized. Because he wanted to experience more "fun." With Billie.

Chapter Five

Tugging the last threads of her dignity around her like a tattered dress, Billie stumbled away from Nick. Even though she held her head high, her legs felt as insecure as her self-esteem. She clenched her hands into tight fists, holding herself together with the last of her willpower. She felt her hopes and dreams break apart, exploding inside her.

Nick's electrifying kiss had knocked her for a loop—an emotional one. The impact had been as physical as if they'd made love. His kiss had been more powerful, more moving, than the one she'd held in her heart all these years, the one she'd remembered in her daydreams and deepened in her sleep. That kiss, so many years ago, had been instigated by her, and she hadn't detected much of a response from Nick, other than surprise.

But this one! This time, *he* had kissed her. *He* had held her in his arms. *He* had taken her mouth like an army storming a cliff. And she'd surrendered! She'd responded like a woman, not in love with another man, not engaged to another man, but as a woman in love with *Nick*. That hot, stirring kiss had rocked her senses, shaken her steady world and shown her the heartbreaking, soul-shattering truth.

She wasn't over Nick. She doubted if she'd ever be.

The horrifying reality slammed against her heart, and her blood began to simmer and boil. For some reason she couldn't understand, that damned kiss had meant everything to her. All at once it had expanded her world and narrowed her focus. Her heart beat for Nick. Her fantasies and hopes were wrapped around him. Today he'd unleashed what she'd been holding inside her heart for so long.

What made tears scald the backs of her eyes was the painful realization that the kiss had meant nothing to him. Nothing! It had been a test! A damn test! One she'd failed miserably.

Damn him! Damn Nick Latham!

Her steps felt stiff and uncertain as she retreated into the house. At least nothing inside reminded her of Nick. Nothing in it suited him. Grateful for that, she drew an insufficient breath into her tight lungs and hugged herself. Tremors of regret, shame and humiliation shuddered through her.

Nick's taste, touch and smell had been branded in her mind, seared into her heart and burned into the fibers of her body. She didn't need reminders of him. She couldn't get away from him, because he was a part of her soul. She'd tasted his hot wildness. She'd absorbed his scent, his spicy cologne, until it filled her pores and made her nerve endings tingle. Hot tears burned her eyes, and she squeezed them back, cursed herself for being a fool.

A shiver ripped through her body, and she trembled from the effort of holding her emotions inside. She knew in that moment that she couldn't stay here. She had to leave before it was too late. Before she lost her heart all over again to Nick. She wouldn't allow her feelings to be trampled by him. She had her pride. Or at least pieces of it left.

Her starchy resolve patched together the threads of her dignity. Without any hesitation, she headed straight for the phone. So what if Nick didn't want her? Doug Schaeffer did. She'd go back home and marry him.

Well, he'd done it. Now he had to fix it. But how?

Nick paced along the side of the pool, Buddy's worried gaze following him. The dog panted in the shade. Sweat trickled down Nick's back, plastering his shirt to his skin. The heat came not so much from the sun's rays but from the heat raging inside him.

Okay, he could admit it. He wanted Billie. Why shouldn't he? She was a beautiful woman. He was a red-blooded American male. But that didn't make it right. And he knew instinctively there was something more. But he couldn't face that.

If he was smart, he'd give himself a good dunking in the chilly pool and douse the desire igniting his blood like a match to a bomb's fuse. But he wasn't smart enough to know what was best for Billie or for himself. Maybe he was more like a kamikaze pilot.

He navigated the pool and headed inside. His target— Billie. His boot heels resounded off the hardwood floor as he cursed himself with each foolish step. Her cavalier attitude ticked him off. He wondered how she could kiss him that way, melt into him like butter, then deny it had meant anything.

What did it mean? Nothing, he told himself. Absolutely nothing. But he knew better. What *else* could it possibly mean? Maybe she was fooling herself. If she was, then he had to know it. Because that was just another reason she shouldn't marry Doug "Blockhead" Schaeffer.

He found her in the kitchen, slouching in a chair at the table. Her shoulders were slumped forward. Her face was turned away from him. She held the phone receiver between her hands, as if studying its contours.

"What do you mean, you were just having fun?" he asked, his voice recoiling like a shotgun blast in the quiet of the room.

Her spine straightened immediately, and she clunked the phone back in its cradle.

"Do you go around kissing men like that? Just for the heck of it?" His crossed arms complemented the frown darkening his features.

She swiveled in her seat and faced him, her eyes narrowed to icy blue chips. A frown drew her brows together into a sharp slant. He would have expected her to be angry at his remark until he noticed she looked pale as chalk dust.

He took a step forward, concern silencing his anger, humiliation and frustration. "What's wrong?"

"I called home," she said, glancing at the phone again, "to see how everything was going. To make sure Doug and the Jacobson kid were handling everything."

Dreading her answer, expecting the worst case scenario, his concerns over why she'd been able to kiss him so thoroughly took a back seat. "And?"

"And they're not." She braced her hands on her thighs and pushed to a standing position.

Suddenly, Billie looked far older than her twenty-three years. Her shoulders squared as if accustomed to the weight of responsibility. Before his very eyes, the vulnerability of the little girl he'd once known shriveled. In its place stood a strong, capable woman, ready to tackle any hurdle put in her way. In her steady, steely gaze, he recognized himself.

"I've got to head back." Her tone terminated the foolish discussion of their kiss.

Knowing he'd drive her back without her even asking and that he'd stay and help mop up whatever mess Schaeffer had caused, he asked, "What happened?"

She raked her fingers through her gold-spun hair. The ends fell like a silky curtain to the round of her shoulders. He wanted to draw her into his embrace, hold her close, lift the burden off her shoulders. But he knew she'd resent him if he tried. And he felt limited in what he could offer her. Instead, he curled his fingers into fists and watched her pace forward a few steps and stop.

"I knew I shouldn't have left. This was a mistake. Right from the start. I should have known." She turned to face him. "Look, you don't have to take me back. You've got your own business to take care of. I can ride the bus or rent a car. I don't want you to feel obligated or—"

"Don't you think you should tell me what happened? And let me decide for myself?"

Her mouth tightened. Her gaze collided with his. "Fine. Kevin Jacobson—you know, Harold's youngest boy—was going to feed and bail hay for me. When he went down to the barn this afternoon, he noticed two of the bulls missing. They'd gotten out of the pen and into the pasture."

"So? What's the big deal?"

"They were with about thirty heifers." She gave him a put-two-and-two-together look.

"Damn."

"Exactly. Those heifers weren't supposed to be bred until next year. They're old enough, according to most ranchers. But since these are mature bulls, I wanted the heifers to have an extra year's growth. So they wouldn't have so much trouble calving."

"So the bulls were a little randy. No use crying over spilt milk, er…" He felt a smile tug at his mouth. "No pun intended."

Her eyes flashed like summer lightning. "In nine months' time, there won't be any humor in the situation when I have to pull a bunch of calves from their mamas."

"But that's no reason to head back now," he said. "You just got here."

"That's not all of it."

Nick crossed his arms, waiting for the punch line. "Go on."

"Kevin tried to get the bulls out of the pasture by himself. He got kicked for his trouble. He's not hurt bad, just a good bruise on his hip. But then he called Doug at work."

Nick shook his head. "Mistake number one."

"Yeah, well, Doug had a few choice words to say about the incident. He helped Jacobson move the bulls back to their own pen. It took them three hours." She glanced at Nick then. Weariness clouded her eyes, making them gunmetal gray. "He ruined his suit…and shoes. He wasted the whole afternoon—"

Tipping his head back, Nick let loose the laugh he'd held inside. The sound burst into the room like a demolition ball knocking down a wall.

"Nick, this is not funny." She glared at him, her hands crossed over her chest. "Doug insisted I return immediately. I'm needed."

He kept on laughing until his sides pinched his ribs. "Think about it, Billie. This is the funniest damn thing."

"Nick." Her voice hardened, then cracked. "It is not." Her mouth quirked. A small, barely noticeable grin emerged then vanished. But it was there, like the sun peeking through a haze of clouds.

Struggling to contain his laughter, he felt his jaw work, his mouth compress. "Can you see Schaeffer...chasing after those bulls? In his pinstripe! With a big ol' stick. Beating those ornery bulls...when all they wanted was—"

She tried to suppress a chuckle, rolling her lips together, but it slipped past. Her face reddened and twisted in an attempt to curb her amusement. Her shoulders shook.

"I can see his face now. Red, hot, peppered with sweat." Nick's sides ached. "I bet for the first time in his pampered life he smelled like manure. Hell, I'd drive you back right now, just to get a look at that picture."

Billie's throaty laugh joined his. "I'm sure he's showered by now."

"Two or three times."

Billie put a hand over her mouth, but her eyes still crinkled with humor. "Nick..." She sucked in a breath. "We shouldn't be laughing. This is serious."

He stumbled toward her and placed an arm around her shoulders, an appeal to join him. "Yeah."

"Doug wasn't laughing." Her eyes sparkled with mischief and stirred something inside him, something hot, something intense. He felt the curve of her breast against his side. His laughter subsided. "He asked me to come home."

"And you're gonna run on back? That's the worst thing you could do." He couldn't let her go back. Not now. Not yet. "The emergency is over. Schaeffer's angry, sure. But he learned a powerful lesson today."

"Which was? Don't get between a bull and his lady friend?" Her mouth twitched with another smile.

His gaze focused on Billie's mouth, her parted lips. His smile dimmed. "No, he learned a little about what you do, day in and day out."

The rest of what he wanted to say caught in his throat. He remembered the soft, sensuous feel of her mouth against his, the sweet, intoxicating taste of her, the feel of her body pressed against him. He wanted to pull her full against him, kiss her, see if his memory was real or imagined. This time, though, he wanted to kiss her slow, excruciatingly slow, taking his time to savor the taste of her.

Slowly, her smile faded, her laughter disintegrated. She sobered, and her gaze became bright, direct. A blush stole its way up her neck and splashed crimson color against her cheeks. "Maybe you're right," she said, her voice husky.

His gut clenched with anticipation. His hand tightened on her arm. Had she read his mind? Did she want the same thing? Maybe if he kissed her again, it wouldn't prove as mind-blowing as the last. Maybe it would be disappointing. But he doubted it. Anticipating another taste of her, he felt his heart pound like a jackhammer in his ears.

"About what?" he drawled.

She gave him a quizzical look. "Doug."

A moment of silence swelled between them, the air simmering with an electrical current that seemed to pull them closer...closer. He felt her warm breath. The pulse at the base of her throat jumped. Her warm, musky scent wrapped around him like an embrace. She looked up at him, her eyes widening, softening. Her gaze shifted to his mouth. Her tongue darted out and licked her lips, leaving a trail of moisture along the pink curve. She wanted him, all right, wanted him as much as he wanted her.

That made him take a step back. What the hell was he doing? This was Billie the Kid. Not some woman he'd just met. He knew her. He knew her family. Where could this lead? Nowhere but trouble. What if something happened between them? Then what? If his ex-wife was right, then he'd manage to screw it up. Then, he'd hurt Billie. And her family. He couldn't accept that. He wouldn't be responsible for hurting her, disappointing her more than she'd already been wounded by the losses in her life. He simply felt responsible for her. He wasn't in love with her.

"Come on," he said, his voice sounding harsh. "Let's go."

She blinked, the heat in her eyes cooling. "Where?"

He wasn't quite sure. Anywhere. He needed breathing room. He needed to step away. He sure as heck didn't need to kiss her again. But he wasn't willing to take her back to Bonnet yet. He wanted her here—away from Schaeffer—until he figured out why she wanted to marry that jerk.

"Shopping," he answered. "Isn't that what you came here for?"

Shopping was at the bottom of her priority list. She needed to go home, and not just to help Doug and the Jacobson kid. More importantly, she needed to get away from Nick. She felt mired in a losing battle of wanting, needing him. With no hope of satisfaction in sight.

But maybe, just maybe, she was wrong.

She'd sensed a chemical reaction, like liquid hydrogen and oxygen combining to make an impressive explosion. The combustible situation could blow up in her face. Could Nick be affected by her? Could he feel the attraction? Could he have *lied* about testing her?

He'd been staring at her mouth. Had he thought of kissing her again, the way she'd thought of kissing him? She wished she had more experience in this sort of thing to know for sure. At that moment she felt painfully aware of her inexperience.

Her immediate reaction was a flat-out denial. But a part of her, a deeply feminine part, gave her new insight, a new awareness, a sharper understanding. A wave of pure excitement washed through her and made her insides ripple.

Still, old doubts resurfaced. "But don't you think—"

"Whenever *you* choose to go back, you can't go back empty-handed." Nick's tone sounded calm and rational compared to her erratic heartbeat that warned her she was getting herself deeper and deeper in trouble. "You told Schaeffer you were going to shop. And that's what you're going to do."

"I'm needed at the ranch," she protested.

"For what?" He grabbed his keys off the counter. "Didn't they get the bulls out of the pasture?"

"Yes, but—"

"The damage has already been done. Nothing you can do about it now."

Maybe he didn't want her to leave. Maybe Nick wanted her to stay. A tiny bud of hope blossomed inside her. "Nick—"

"What?" he interrupted. "Look, didn't you hear what Doug said at dinner the other night? He thinks any kid can handle your job. You want him to go on thinking that? If you do, then you're not the Billie I remember. If you don't, then stay here. With me.''

Did she detect an invitation in that sandpaper-roughened tone? Oh, how she wanted to believe he wanted her! Was that simply her ego wanting something she'd never had? Or was it her heart? Could Nick ever be attracted to her, not as Billie the Kid, but as Billie Rae Gunther?

"Let Schaeffer suffer—I mean, experience—running a ranch.''

Did Nick *want* her to stay to keep her away from Doug or to keep her for himself? Her pulse quickened. She glanced at his mouth, remembering the roughness, the gentleness, the power he had to liquefy her bones.

Part of her wanted to push him, test him, see if he'd kiss her again. Was there truly something—anything—between them? Before she turned around and married Doug. "But what if something else—''

"They'll be fine. Relax, will you?'' He put a hand against the small of her back and gently pushed her toward the back door. How the heck could she relax with him near her, touching her, having kissed her? "What else could happen?''

More than a few possibilities shot through her mind. None of which related to the Rocking G. All of her ideas were steamy, sexy and too tempting to ignore. She couldn't leave Houston. She couldn't leave until she figured out what was going on between her and Nick. Part of her prayed it was nothing, because she didn't know if her heart would survive his rejection again. But part of her dared to hope something might be blooming. If so, then she couldn't rest until she knew for certain. She had to test that gut feeling, that awakening feminine voice inside her.

What better way than to show Nick she was all woman beneath her work shirt and jeans?

"Where are you going?" Nick asked, dragging his feet through the Galleria as Billie tugged on his arm.

"Over here. Didn't you tell Doug I should pick out something nice for our honeymoon? You weren't thinking of a new pair of cowboy boots, were you?"

"I guess not." He frowned.

She pulled him into the lingerie boutique. The scent of honeysuckle and roses assaulted him and made his nose twitch. This was dangerous, he thought. Red, hot and dangerous.

He jammed his hands into his pockets. He knew better than to touch anything. Especially Billie.

"Anything I can help you with?" a woman asked, giving Nick a once-over with her thickly mascaraed eyes. "Are you looking for anything in particular?"

"No," Nick said, his gaze swerving back to Billie. "Just browsing."

"Do you have anything for a wedding night?" Billie asked.

"Oh, sure!" The saleswoman's dark eyes snapped with sudden enthusiasm. "Congratulations, by the way." Her gaze lingered on Nick, making him uncomfortable.

"Thanks," Billie said.

"You'll want to take a look at the nightgowns along the wall over there." The woman pointed to her left.

Billie hooked her arm through Nick's. "You'll have to help me pick something really sexy. Something a bridegroom would like."

Mistake number two, he thought, standing between two racks of slinky, sexy lingerie and watching Billie. Her brow furrowed as she meandered through the store, her fingers grazing silk nightgowns, skimming over satin teddies. He wondered what it would feel like to have her smooth her hands over his bare skin. He ground his teeth in frustration.

Don't think about it! Just don't think about it.

He tried to distract himself with the saleswoman, who kept eyeing him across the room. But he only ended up comparing her to Billie. And there was really no comparison. Billie had a natural beauty. She didn't need enhancements like unnatural blush pinkening her cheeks, dark eyeliner accenting her blue eyes or bright red lipstick showing off her sensuous mouth. She had a flush of sun on her tanned cheeks, a genuine sparkle in her eye and a rosy hue to her lips that made him think of passionate kisses and moans of pleasure.

She pulled something lacy off the metal rack and moved toward him. A smile lurked on her lips. "What the heck is this for?"

He stared at the red garter belt. She twirled it around her index finger then popped him on the arm with the elastic band. He imagined her wearing it, the lace hugging her slim hips and shimmering hose accenting her long, shapely legs. His mouth went bone-dry.

"Who'd want to wear this, anyway? It looks about as comfortable as a rubber band." She turned and grabbed another item off a tableful of silk panties. "And look at these!" She held up a white thong bikini. "Why would anybody in their right mind wear this? What's the point? Why bother with anything at all?"

His throat tightened as he attempted to swallow. "Billie," he almost groaned, "it's not necessarily for comfort."

"Oh, yeah. Right. It's for you guys." She handed him the silk thong. "Well, no thank you. I prefer cotton. Not

all this stuff. And if Doug doesn't like it, then he can..."
Her gaze cut toward him. "Do *you* like these kinds of
things?" A seductive tone, one he'd never heard from
her, crept into her voice and made heat flare inside him.

A risky topic, he thought. He crumpled the thong in
his fist. "Uh, sometimes. Depends on the woman."

"Hmm." She contemplated his answer, as if consid-
ering the possibilities. He prayed she wouldn't ask him
straight out if she could be one of those women. Because,
dammit, he'd have to say yes.

"When?" She slung the garter belt over her shoulder,
part of it dangled in front of her breast, catching his attention, making sweat pop out on his brow. "You said
you liked these things sometimes. When?"

He forced his gaze back to her face, off the damn garter, off her full breast that made him want to size it with
the palm of his hand. She tipped her head to the side and
studied him as if he were a specimen under the micro-
scope. He shifted from foot to foot. Could she see the
frustration building in him? The need wrapping around
him like a coiled rope?

He shrugged and turned away. "I don't know."

"I bet you do." She caught his arm, her fingers soft,
firm, insistent. "Come on, Nick." She winked. "You can
tell me. We're friends, right?"

Just friends. That's all they'd ever been. But suddenly
he wanted more, much more. He reminded himself that
she wanted Doug. Or did she? With his incoherent
thoughts spiraling, he emphasized, "Yeah, we're
friends."

"Then you'll help me."

He nodded and forced down his reservations in a hard
swallow.

"What would you pick for me to wear on our honeymoon...I mean, on *my* honeymoon."

Nothing, he thought. *Absolutely nothing.* An image of her strong, supple, naked body sprang to mind. As if the honeymoon in question would be spent with him. A smile curved his lips until he realized she was referring to her fiancé's tastes.

What should she wear for Doug? An old-fashioned flannel nightgown that buttoned at her neck and touched the tips of her toes. That would be more appropriate. Maybe chastity belts were back in fashion. Could he convince Billie that her fiancé would prefer something less risqué? He doubted it. She wasn't that naive. Still, where were those granny gowns?

Turning away from her and his inappropriate thoughts, he filed through a rack of negligees, the plastic hangers clapping together in his hurry to get this unpleasant task over with. He looked at virginal white gowns, racy reds, bold and daring blacks. Some had peekaboo lace across the front, some dipped low in the back, others had thigh-high slits. He imagined Billie wearing each one, and his blood heated.

None were appropriate for her to wear in front of Schaeffer.

"What do you think about this?" Billie asked, drawing his attention away from the rows and rows of gowns.

She held a white gauzy material in front of her, pinching it in at the waist. She twirled around, the skirt flared, the uneven hem showing off her snug blue jeans, giving glimpses of her firm thighs and putting his imagination into overdrive. She wobbled in her less-than-graceful move, and it opened his heart more to this woman who still had a touch of girlhood charm. In his mind's eye he could see her in this shimmery cloud moving toward him, her skin flushed, her lips parted, her hair tousled and sexy.

"Well?" she prodded.

He wanted to say no. But how could he lie? She'd look stunning in it. A flare of jealousy flashed inside him. His hands curled into fists at his sides. He'd deck Schaeffer if Mr. Fancy Pants ever got a look at Billie wearing this.

"Won't you get cold?" he asked, trying to discourage her.

She blinked. "Not if this works right."

His thoughts took an abrupt detour as he imagined Billie walking toward Schaeffer, willingly going into his arms, lifting her face for an intimate kiss. Hot fissures erupted down his spine. Would she kiss Schaeffer the way she'd kissed him? He blocked out the image, the questions. But the confusion remained. His gut felt like he'd swallowed a bucket of nuts and bolts.

Billie deserved better than slick-talking, fast-tracking Doug who wore suits and ties, not jeans and boots, and treated her like a prized poodle. She deserved to be treated like a woman, a flesh and blood woman with wants and needs and desires as strong as any man's. He couldn't—wouldn't—imagine her wearing sexy lingerie for Schaeffer...or anyone else...but him.

That was the most dangerous thought he'd ever entertained. Somehow he had to wrestle his urges under control. Because he sure wasn't the man to make Billie feel like a woman. Hadn't his ex-wife told him precisely how he'd failed?

But maybe he could show Billie how a woman should be treated. Even if he wasn't a so-called master, he sure as hell had to be better than Schaeffer.

Chapter Six

This was not what she'd bargained for! Why couldn't she be graceful for once? Billie'd wanted to show Nick she was as feminine as the next woman, but she didn't want to *show* him everything. And this negligee would definitely show *everything!*

With his intense stare focused on her, Billie felt suddenly vulnerable, as if her jeans and cotton shirt had melted away and she stood before him naked as the day she was born. Her temperature climbed steadily to a boiling point. He didn't have to answer her question about whether he liked it or not. Even lacking experience with men, she knew. It felt as though her sixth sense, or maybe it was her womanly intuition, had shifted suddenly into high gear when it had been idling for most of her life. Nick liked the gauzy gown she held against her. And he liked it a lot!

The thin cotton material flowed over her and made her curves look softer, more sensual. Against her bare arms and fingertips it felt luxuriant, like a soft, supple second skin.

"I think I'll get this one," she said, her throat constricted by a need she didn't quite understand or want to acknowledge. She slanted her gaze away from the hard-edged, burning intensity of his amber eyes.

"Shouldn't you try it on?" he asked, his voice deep, husky, almost an invitation.

Her cheeks burned at the thought, and her skin tightened like wet leather. "What?" Her gaze darted around the busy store. "You mean, here? In front of you!"

He chuckled. "I'm sure they have a dressing room."

"Oh." Was that disappointment filtering through her?

"I'll even offer my assistance and personal opinion." His mouth quirked, pulling to the side, and making the groove along his cheek deepen. He'd successfully turned the tables on her little charade. "Free of charge."

His teasing manner grated on her nerves like sandpaper. Maybe she'd misread his intensity. It hadn't been interest, desire or need. She wished for one minute that he wasn't kidding her as he'd so often razzed her during their adolescent years. "No, thanks. I mean, no, it's not necessary. I'm sure this will fit."

"You have the right size?" he asked.

She rolled her eyes. "Sheesh! It's not nice to ask a woman—any woman—whether it's your mother, wife or little tomboy sister, about her size. Besides, Doug won't mind if it's too big or even too small. It's not like I'm going to wear it out in public. It'll be just for *him*." She said it in hopes of sparing her pride, hoping it might dig into Nick just a little. "If you know what I mean. And I doubt I'll have to wear it for long."

A wince made his eyes darken like dusk and told her she'd hit her mark. With her confidence slowly recovering, she swiveled about on her boot heel and headed for the checkout counter.

A thought almost tripped her up. Was he watching her? Her spine tensed and her legs felt wooden. She almost groaned at the thought that she probably walked like an old cowhand, rather than a woman. Why had she worn these boots? With a quick glance over her shoulder to test her newly acquired sixth sense, she caught Nick staring after her. His gaze was like a bold caress. It gave her a surge of feminine pride, a heady sensation of power, a power she somehow held over Nick.

Then she felt her toe catch on something and she stumbled forward, managing to catch her balance before sprawling across the floor. She cursed. But she didn't look back. She felt her face growing warm.

Maybe, just maybe, Nick hadn't been teasing her earlier. But it was hard to tell. She'd never felt this way with Doug. His compliments were more like double-edged swords. His condescending tone and superior attitude had kept her feeling insecure rather than boosting her confidence. She'd excused his behavior with the knowledge that he did know more about fashion than she did. Several of his predictable remarks saturated her mind like poison. "You look great tonight, babe," he'd said, giving her the usual predate scrutiny as he brushed a stray hair into place or flicked a piece of lint off her dress. "The Sterlings will be impressed with my choice of a fiancée." Why did it seem like a compliment aimed more at himself than her?

All it took from Nick, though, was a simple look that gave off enough electricity to light up Houston during a hurricane. With his dark, compelling eyes and warm, lazy smile, he made her feel centered in a spotlight. He made her feel uncomfortable inside her own skin, like a woman. His gaze produced a sultry blush surface along her skin, tingling her nerve endings. She didn't know how the heck to respond, so she'd run the other way.

Waiting as the cashier folded the gown in tissue paper, Billie noticed a bottle of sweet-smelling cologne on the counter. After testing it on the inside of her wrist, she gave the bottle to the cashier to add to her bill. When had she ever been so extravagant, spending money on silly clothes and foolish dreams? Guilt inched through her, not for the expenditures, but because she was buying these things for Nick. To garner his attention. Not her fiancé's.

She'd never felt particularly attractive to Doug. But Nick! He made her feel alive. He made her feel like a real woman, with real needs, natural desires.

These crazy thoughts were dangerous, but right now she didn't care. She was willing to play with fire…to be near Nick. This one last time. She considered this fantasy week her own version of a bachelorette party, her last hurrah, before she settled down…with Doug.

"I'll get that," Nick said suddenly from beside her.

The cashier's eyes widened. "Certainly, sir."

"It's not necessary," Billie said, her lips compressed into a thin line. She pushed her credit card toward the woman.

Nick took it and stuck it back in Billie's wallet, replacing it with his gold card. "I insist. I promised you I'd foot the bill." He gave her a sexy wink that made her toes curl. "It's my pleasure."

Feeling the cashier's curious gaze shift back and forth between them, Billie didn't say another word. She put away her wallet and waited for Nick outside.

"You made us sound like lovers!" Her voice sounded breathless when he met her outside the boutique. She wasn't sure if she was angry, flattered or just plain frustrated at her endless hoping that Nick would become her lover.

He shrugged as if it didn't concern him. "Better than a big brother buying a nightgown for his little sister." He put a casual arm around her shoulders and pulled her with him into the flow of traffic meandering through the mall. "Come on. Thought we'd look for a couple of dresses for you." He led her through the mall to an expensive department store. "I'm sure you'll need them for wedding showers and such."

After a couple of hours, shopping for less intimate apparel, and keeping the conversation neutral, away from honeymoons and the hot kiss they'd shared by his pool, they stopped for a bite to eat at a local Italian restaurant. But Billie's mind dwelled on what it would be like to be Nick's lover.

Would he be gentle, demanding, tender, driven? What would it feel like to snuggle against his side, have him whisper silly things in her ear? A piercing need seized her like a fist around her heart. She wanted to know those intimacies more than anything. But she never would.

Hidden with her in a back corner booth, Nick poured another glass of Chianti for each of them. Passionate violin music set the stage for a romantic dinner for two and twisted Billie's insides into a nervous knot. This was definitely a setting for lovers, and she felt like an imposter.

Soft candlelight accented golden highlights in Nick's honey-colored hair and his sun-bronzed tan. Unable to wander away from him as she had in the department store, she fiddled with her red-and-white-checkered napkin. She wondered what he was thinking.

The waitress set two heaping platters of pasta between them. Nick did the honors, scooping up a generous portion of each and setting a plate in front of her. The creamy fettuccine Alfredo tasted rich and decadent. The thin spaghetti, dipped in a tomato basil sauce, reminded her of delicate angels' wings.

Feeling shy and unsure, Billie concentrated on not slurping her spaghetti. In her head, she heard her mother's voice, "If you want to catch a boy, Billie, then you have to play the game." How many times had Billie rolled her eyes at that one? She'd never been one to play "the game." She'd never quite understood the rules. And besides she hadn't wanted *any* boy. She'd always wanted Nick.

Now she tried desperately to remember what other detailed advice her mother had given her, but the sage words flitted out of her grasp like a feather in the wind. The silence between them seemed as awkward and uncomfortable as in-laws trailing along on their daughter's honeymoon. The noise in the restaurant ebbed, the laughter at other tables fading. Her pulse raced, roaring in her ears, and she accidentally clunked her fork against the plate.

"Sorry," she mumbled around a mouthful of pasta.

He gave her a half smile and tasted his wine.

Remembering his kiss, the feel of his mouth against hers, she swallowed hard and tried to think of something else...anything besides Nick. "How was work today?"

"Work?" His fork paused between his plate and mouth. "Fine."

"Good."

He chewed thoughtfully for a moment then added, "I'll be gone most of tomorrow. But you can use my extra car."

"Okay." She nodded. Disappointment sifted through her. Irritated at her response, she reminded herself that

Nick wasn't her baby-sitter. He had a company to run. "What will you be doing?"

"The usual assortment of things."

"Like what?" she asked, realizing she didn't really know what Nick did, how he ran his company, how the construction business worked.

He shrugged, as if it wasn't important. "I have to check the progress at each of the sites. Then there's a meeting with a builder. We're going to look at some plans for a residential area. We may handle the streets, water, that sort of thing."

"Do you come up with the plans yourself?" she asked, remembering he had an engineering degree.

"I work with the architect. Together, we figure out what's plausible with the layout of the land."

"And you mostly build roads?"

"Up until now. But we're expanding. There's so much building going on in Houston. We're contracting out different sites. If you want, I could show you a bridge we're working on. Then there's a project with the city. We're widening a couple of roads near here. Getting involved with this builder will really help. I want to steer the company into developing." A gleam in his eyes sparked an idea inside her.

She wanted to spend more time with Nick, hard as it might be later to leave without him, and she wanted to see where he worked, what he did, how he spent his days. Smiling, she said in a Mae West voice, "I've shown you mine. Now it's time you showed me yours."

His startled gaze made her laugh.

"Your office," she added. "Your construction sites. I showed you what I do, now you show me where you work."

He set his fork on the edge of his plate and studied her for a minute. "You really want to see that?"

"Yes."

A frown dented the space between his brows. "Why?" He shook his head. "I mean, it's muddy...loud...."

"So? My boots have been in worse than a mud puddle and cattle aren't exactly quiet when they're put through a chute." Her chest tightened when she realized why Nick might be reluctant. She glanced down at her napkin. "If you'd rather I not go, I understand. I didn't mean to—"

"No." He offered an apologetic smile and put a reassuring hand on hers.

Their gazes met. As if a charge from a cattle prod had shocked them both, they glanced away. He concentrated on his wine. She twirled her pasta around her fork. Suddenly her fingers felt awkward, as clumsy as her attempt to capture Nick's interest at the lingerie boutique. She'd been foolish to try.

"I'd like for you to come, Billie. Sure. It'll be fun. It surprised me, is all, that you'd want to see what I do. It might bore you out of your mind."

Bore her? How would spending time with Nick bore her? Jumping at the chance, she asked, "What time do we start?"

"Early."

"Not a problem. I'm a rancher. I'm used to the crack of dawn. That's when cattle like to eat and calves like to be born. Just give me a cup of coffee and I'll be rarin' to go."

As if amazed at her eagerness, he shook his head and rubbed his jaw. "Okay. If that's the way you really want to spend your day."

She couldn't think of anything more promising.

* * *

"Oo-oh, baby! Welcome to my life!"

The shrill whistle that followed acted like an ice cube down Nick's back. He snapped his head in the direction of the shirtless construction worker who dared a wolf call aimed at Billie. The next comment died on the man's lips when he saw the rage burning in his boss's stare. The man lowered his hard hat and muttered a quick apology, turning as Billie and Nick passed. Aware of the too eager male eyes following them and too attentive himself to the way Billie's jeans clung to her hips and long legs, Nick led her up the steps of the trailer and out of sight of the crew. They turned and looked out over the site.

"You were right," Billie said over the ruckus of a jackhammer. Her eyes sparkled like the clear sky. "It is loud."

He frowned, thinking his crew's appreciation of her was more obnoxious than the bulldozer's grinding gears. He put his hand on the doorknob, squeezing his irritation out of his system. There wasn't anything to be upset with. Billie was a beautiful woman. What man wouldn't notice? He should have anticipated his crew's enthusiasm over her arrival.

"Friendly, aren't they?" she added, slipping him a sly smile.

"Didn't think they'd be your type," he said.

She tilted her head and stared up at him, her eyes squinting against the glare of the sun. "How come?"

"Bubba, over there—" he hooked his thumb over his shoulder "—the one ready to carry you to his double-wide castle, is a teddy bear, actually. Probably one of the nicest men you'll ever meet." He gave a pause the length of a heartbeat, then added, "Not anything like your fiancé."

Billie caught the not-too-subtle jab. Instead of her blue eyes turning frosty, they glowed. When had she quit being defensive of Schaeffer? Instead of encouraging him, that he might be making progress, it made his nerves as brittle as shale.

"If you're interested," he suggested, giving the eighteen-year-old with the grating whistle another glance, "I could set you up a date for later."

"Thanks," she said, her tone sultry as the humidity, her eyes gleaming with amusement. "But I'm all booked."

He cocked an eyebrow in question.

"With you." Her grin broadened, and she jabbed him in the ribs with her elbow. Her smile faltered then. "Remember? *You* promised you'd take me out on the town and show me the time of my life. When did you plan that to happen? I can't wait around forever. Not with other offers pouring in."

"Tonight." He put his hand to her back, hoping she'd go on into the trailer.

She didn't. "If it's too much trouble," she added, "I could see if Bubba, over there, has a free night this week."

Nick matched her confident grin with his own cocky version. He wouldn't let her see how uncomfortable it made him to think of her out with *any* man. Yet, it made him twice as nervous to take her out himself. But he'd play his trump card to get the wedding stopped. "Bubba's not available. The ladies all love him. He's got more dates than days of the week. So, I guess you're stuck with me. And after our date, you won't ever want to see Schaeffer again." He gave her a slight nudge with his hand. "You might want me instead."

Startled by his foolish comment, he shifted from foot

to foot. When he jerked open the trailer door, his gaze met hers. The color of her eyes deepened to indigo and tattooed his heart with desire.

He hadn't expected to want her to want him. But he did. Damn, if he didn't want her for himself. But, he reminded himself, that wasn't possible. He remembered the crush she'd had on him so long ago. It had tongue-tied him but at the same time boosted his ego. He stared down at her round, solemn eyes and knew her feelings for him had faded with the years. Hadn't she made that clear? But had his affection for her grown, intensified, taken on a whole new meaning?

The hope in his heart shriveled, replaced by sheer panic.

"Maybe. But remember this, Nick, I'm going to marry Doug," she stated. With a decisive flick of her wrist, she brushed the hair off her shoulder and moved past him, entering the trailer.

Her words clattered in his mind and a cold hand fisted his gut. *No way, Billie the Kid. I am not going to let you marry Schaeffer. Not without a fight. Not until I've made damn sure he's the best man.*

But if Schaeffer wasn't the best man for the job of Billie's husband, then who was?

Maybe that was the answer to his dilemma. His panic easing, his confidence returning, Nick figured he could find Billie a substitute groom. Someone she could really fall in love with. Someone who wouldn't take advantage of her. Someone he'd approve. But who?

That stumped him. He glanced back at Bubba and shook his head. No way. He thought of a string of bachelor friends, fraternity brothers, drinking buddies. He knew their thoughts on women, how they treated them, how each of them avoided commitments. Then he scratched them off his list one by one using either character flaws or physical imperfections as reasons.

He followed her inside the site office. The bitter smell of overbrewed coffee and acrid odor of cigarette smoke hung in the cluttered room like a hazy cloud before a downpour. Mud patches smeared the linoleum floor. Dust and grime speckled the windows that looked out over the site. How many times had he been in here and never noticed the piles of papers, the heaps of blueprints, the tool belts left in random places? He knew the only reason he noticed now was because he wanted Billie to be impressed with his work, impressed with him. He also knew his ex-wife would have been as disgusted with his work sites as she had been embarrassed by his too common business.

Billie didn't seem to mind, though. In fact, she looked as if she fit in, with her jeans, T-shirt and cowboy boots. If he lent her a tool belt and hard hat, she'd look like one of the boys. His gaze skimmed over her rounded curves. Nah, she could never again look like one the boys. At least, not to him.

"Hey, Jody," Nick said, grabbing a hard hat near the door and handing it to Billie. He wished it was cold out and he'd offer her a heavy jacket to hide her figure. Not just from the crew, but from him, too. "How's it going?"

Jody Davis glanced up from the plans he studied. His hardened, crusty hands remained on the table, flattening the curling edges of blue-tinted paper. When his gaze landed on Billie, the steel-haired man's face transformed. He straightened, and the papers rattled and rolled into a tubular shape. Jody's chrome-colored gaze traveled over Billie's shapely form, and a slow grin tipped up the corners of his usually stern-set mouth. He stubbed out the butt of his cigarette. "Well, well, who'd you bring for show-and-tell?"

"Put your eyes back in their sockets," Nick said. "This is my little sister, Billie Gunther. Billie, my right-hand man, Jody Davis."

The man's hooded gaze flicked back and forth between Nick and Billie. "Well, hell! So you're Billie the Kid."

"She doesn't go by that nickname anymore," Nick said.

But this time Billie didn't seem to mind, and Jody kept right on talking. "Nick and his pop have talked about you and your family for years. Must say, I'd pictured you different."

Billie shook his rugged hand and smiled. "What'd you expect? A man?"

"Nope. A kid, from the way Latham talked." He rolled his lips inward and gave a low whistle, his gaze appreciating her obvious feminine curves. "You're no kid."

"Glad you noticed. I'm not related to Nick, either. So don't let him give you that big brother routine." She laughed and slanted her eyes toward Nick. "I think I like it around here."

Jody tipped the brim of his hard hat up. "You're welcome anytime…anytime." He pulled a chair around, dusted it with his hand and offered it to Billie. "Want some coffee? A soda?" He leaned toward her and lowered his voice. "Beer's not allowed till quittin' time. But your wish is—"

"Shut up, Davis," Nick grunted, stepping between them. "You're talking to an engaged woman."

"What? An engaged woman can't drink?" Jody rubbed his jaw, the silver whiskers sounding like sandpaper. "So you're getting married? That why Latham shot out of here last Friday like the cops were after him?"

"I don't know about all that," Billie answered Jody's question, humor lacing her words, "but yes, I'm getting married."

Nick felt her eyes on him, studying him. He stared hard out the window. "What the hell is that new kid doing on the grater? He doesn't have enough experience."

Mumbling to himself, Nick grabbed the plans Jody had been studying and bent over the table. Pretending to ignore their lively banter, he spread the coiled papers open and studied the contour map.

This was a mistake, he thought, a bad mistake to bring Billie to this site...any site. He should have left her home, given her a map to the Galleria and ignored her interest in his work. But, hell, he admitted only to himself, her interest in his business had caressed his ego. An ego badly bruised by his ex-wife.

Diane had never shown any interest, except in the checks he brought home at the end of each month. He'd once wanted his wife to share a stake in the company, to feel the enthusiasm he felt when he clenched a deal. But now, he wasn't so sure. Bringing a woman to a site was obviously not a bright idea.

"Where's the lucky groom?" Jody asked.

"Back home."

"And he let you out of his sight?" The middle-aged man shook his head. "That was a mistake."

"Why's that?" Billie asked, toying with the brim of her hard hat.

Jody crossed his arms over his chest. "Well, you're just too much temptation for any man to pass up, darlin', no matter if you're married, engaged or related to this bear of a boss." He punched Nick in the arm. "You her bodyguard then, big brother?"

"You might say that," he mumbled, keeping his focus on the blueprints.

"Nick's determined to stop the wedding," Billie explained.

"Of course." Jody chuckled. "Smart man that he is, Latham probably wants you for himself."

Nick felt a growl of frustration rumble in his throat. "Don't you have something productive to do, Davis? What am I paying you for?"

"Actually," Billie said, ignoring Nick, "it's my fiancé that Nick doesn't like. He just thinks I deserve somebody better."

"I see." Jody tapped a cigarette out of a pack and lit it with a red lighter. He took a deep pull then released a puff of smoke toward the ceiling. "Your fiancé…is he good-looking?"

"Yes." She glanced toward Nick, smiled and said, "Very."

"Makes good dough?"

Her gaze shifted back to Jody, who should go into the matchmaking business, Nick thought. "He's very wealthy." Was that pride he detected in Billie's voice? Or greed? "Runs his own company."

"His daddy's company." A snarl curled Nick's lip.

"Uh-huh." Jody dismissed Nick's comment with a flick of his cigarette, knocking the ashes onto the floor. "Treats you decent?" His gaze narrowed. "No foolin' around with other women. No knockin' you around or anything."

"Of course not! He's an upstanding citizen. A member of the city council."

"That should prove it. He's a damn politician," Nick mumbled.

Jody slapped Nick on the back. "Then it's jealousy. Don't let Latham fool you. He's not as noble as he wants you to think."

He felt Billie studying him. Then her brow arched with that too familiar I-got-one-on-you look that they'd shot back and forth as kids. Unable to back away from her challenge, he met her gaze squarely, denying Jody's foolish words with his own steely eyed stare even though the truth beat in his heart. Her eyes looked as blue, warm and inviting as the Pacific Ocean. A need like none he'd ever known gripped him.

God, it was true. He wanted Billie. He wanted her for himself.

The air around him sucked the breath right out of his lungs. The walls of the trailer closed in on him. Heat coiled in the pit of his stomach, tiny tentacles spreading through him, making him hotter than the pathetic air conditioner in the window could relieve. He grabbed the hard hat he'd given Billie, dusted it off with his forearm and placed it squarely on her head. "Come on, I'll show you around."

She didn't move. "Could be," she said back to Jody, "he thinks I should still date around even though I'm engaged. Even says he'll take me out. But he hasn't yet."

"He hasn't?" Jody frowned. "Well, I'm disappointed in him. You know, I think of Latham, here, like a son. Taught him everything I know."

"Which didn't take long," Nick added.

"What signs should I watch for?" she asked. "That is, to see if he's interested?"

"Shoot, Billie." Jody stubbed out his cigarette with

the heel of his work boot. "Could be anything. He might act a little gruff. Might be irritable."

"Isn't he always?" she asked with a chuckle.

"I don't know about that. Most days he's downright congenial. Maybe it is you." Jody watched him, his silvery eyebrows slanting into a concerned frown. "He is kind of grumpy today."

"It's either that," Billie said, "or PMS."

"There you go!" Jody's shoulders shook with suppressed laughter.

Nick's frown deepened. The muscles along his neck and shoulders pinched. "Are you two finished?"

"No," they said simultaneously. Then they both laughed out loud, their unharmonious pitches ricocheting off the metal ceiling.

"Well, I've had enough." He walked toward the door. "I've got work to do. I'll be back, Billie. You can stay here with Jody if you want."

She kept her attention on his foreman, pushing Nick's frustration to an all-time high. "Nick did buy me a night-gown."

Jody's eyes widened. "Well, well, well. Now, that's interesting."

Nick ducked his head and rubbed his forehead. A headache hammered four-inch nails into his skull. "When you two vultures finish picking me apart, you can find me—"

"Hold on there, buddy. I think I've learned more than I wanted to know here." Jody gave a nod to Billie and tipped the front of his hard hat like a cowboy's Stetson. "Don't want to come between you and your lady, er, friend. So, you show her around." He clapped Nick's shoulder hard. "I'll take care of—"

"Make sure that new kid knows what he's doing. I don't want any accidents."

Jody nodded, gave Billie a friendly, conspiratorial wink, and left.

Billie suppressed a smile, the corners of her mouth pinching her lips into a pucker that looked too inviting and too damn dangerous for Nick's own good. She sat on a wobbly three-legged stool. "Did you ever bring Diane here?"

Her question startled him. "What makes you ask that?"

She shrugged and propped her boot on her opposite knee. "I don't know. You seem pretty defensive, almost territorial of your space. It's a different side of you. You act like you don't want me here."

"Maybe I'm not used to being attacked."

"Ah, Nick, we were just kidding. You can dish it out, but you can't swallow it, huh?" She stood and walked to the table. "So tell me what all these blueprints mean."

Drawing in a calming breath, he moved to her side, tried to ignore the new scent lingering on her sun-warmed skin. She smelled like a beach—warm, fragrant, breezy. Sharpening his senses on the work site, he pointed out the layout of the road construction, how the plans fit, the contours of the land, the machines used to do the work.

When he glanced back at her, she was smiling, her eyes sparkling like sun off water. "You really love your work, don't you?"

He nodded, feeling his throat tighten. "This part."

"What do you mean?"

He plopped onto the stool Billie had vacated, nearly tipping himself over. Righting himself, he rested his elbows on his knees. He'd revealed too much, but somehow he knew Billie of all people would understand. "I don't know really. Just something I've been struggling with lately.''

She leaned her hip against the table and waited for him to continue. He sorted through his thoughts and tried to articulate what had been bothering him. "If I could do this, stay here, work at the site, manage the equipment, do the work, see the progress firsthand, then, yeah, I'd love my job."

"Isn't that what you do?"

"Not anymore. Most of my time is spent getting permits, meeting with potential clients. Hell, I'm more like Schaeffer than I thought."

She laughed. "I don't think you have anything to worry about there."

He searched her eyes for the truth. He wished he could believe that. God, he wanted to know she thought more of him than Schaeffer. Treading in dangerous waters, he glanced at his watch and stood. "I've got a meeting to get to. Come on, you can come, too."

"Afraid to leave me here with Jody and the boys?"

"You bet. They'd waste the afternoon chasing you around the trailer."

"Might be fun." She headed toward the door. "Do I need this?" She pointed to the hard hat.

"Not anymore. Not where we're going." He grabbed a tie off a hook by the door and slipped it around his neck. "We're going corporate."

She glanced down at her attire. "Like this?"

"You look great. You'll be my lethal weapon."

"How's that?"

"You'll distract them. While I clench the deal."

"I'm not sure that's a sound plan."

"I am," he said, having no doubts about her abilities. A shout drew their attention out the window. Jody yelled at a crew member, his face reddened by heat and anger.

"He's really something," she said.

"He's something, all right. Maybe unemployed would be a good description."

"Ah, Nick. We were just kidding." She placed a hand on his arm, the warmth and companionship turning into a sexy heat. "Don't worry. I know you're not interested in me. I've always known that. You're just looking out for me. Like Jake would have."

He grabbed her arms, tightened his fingers around her taut muscles, pulled her close to his chest. He wanted to kiss her, show her she was wrong. He did want her. That was the problem. "Billie—"

Her eyes widened. Her mouth softened into an *O*. She looked like she'd welcome his kiss. His throat clogged like a stopped-up drainpipe. Emotions he didn't recognize, he didn't know he owned, choked him.

"What is it, Nick?"

He shook loose the odd need that had a hold on his heart. He didn't need Billie. He didn't need any woman. And, according to his ex-wife, he didn't know how to treat one anyway. He wasn't the right man for Billie. But he knew then, way down deep where he couldn't deny it any longer, that he wanted to be the right one for her. He wanted it more than anything.

Shaking his head, he rasped, "You're right, Billie." Slowly he loosened his hold on her. "I'm trying to protect you from Schaeffer."

And me.

Chapter Seven

Late that afternoon, the phone was ringing when they walked back into Nick's house.

"Let the answering machine pick up," Nick said. "If it's important, Jody knows to beep me." He knelt and greeted Buddy. The excited retriever waggled his silky long tail, making his back end teeter then bobble and his nails click and slide on the hardwood floor.

Billie grabbed a glass from the cabinet. A heavy-handed silence had settled between her and Nick after leaving downtown Houston. Feeling like a country bumpkin, she'd tagged along to his meeting. Unable to keep her mouth shut, she'd made a couple of suggestions the client hadn't considered. Nick had clenched the deal and hugged her on the way out the door.

"You make a great partner," he'd said.

Although she'd tried to match his smile and enthusiasm, she'd felt a part of her crumple. She would never be a lover to Nick. He'd never see her that way. He only saw her as a "partner" or as a "buddy."

The drive home had given her time to analyze her thoughts and feelings. And left her more confused than ever. What had she experienced between them when he'd grabbed her in the trailer, pulled her close?

She'd thought he was going to kiss her. She'd *wanted* him to kiss her. Wanted it with every fiber in her body. But he hadn't pressed his mouth to hers. In fact, it felt as if a solid, concrete barrier had come between them.

It was as if he'd wanted to say something, to bridge the gap separating them, but at the last minute he'd latched on to the safe big brother role. Or maybe she was trying to read things into what he said and, more importantly, what he didn't say.

With the phone still ringing, Nick took the dog outside. Ignoring the urge to answer it, Billie filled a glass with water from the refrigerator. The chilly air cooled her heated thoughts and expectations about Nick. She had to get a grip on reality. Nick wasn't interested in her. And she didn't want him to be. But she did want him to see her as a woman, not a buddy. It had more to do with pride, she figured, than matters of the heart.

But part of her heart began to crack. Who was she fooling?

After the answering machine replayed Nick's succinct message, a high-pitched beep sounded and an angry voice crackled in the phone speaker. "Billie, you there? Pick up. Pick up now. This is an emergency."

With her heart in her throat, she lunged for the phone, spilling the water down her front. A roar of panic sounded in her ears. Her blood felt cold and hard like ice cubes. "Doug? What is it? What's happened?"

"Come home. Right away."

Visions exploded in her head. Was it her mother? Was she hurt? Sick? Oh, God, she felt fear crumple her steely independence like an aluminum can. Her knuckles turned white as she clutched the phone to her ear. "What—"

"That irresponsible, no-good Jacobson quit today. I knew we couldn't rely on him."

She shook her head. "Doug, is my mother all right?"

"Your mother?" he asked. She pictured a sneer curling his upper lip. "What do you want? Me to take care of her, too? I've got enough troubles taking care of these damn cows."

Anger, hot and fierce, stiffened her spine. "This emergency is about the hired help quitting?"

"Yeah, what did you think? I've been breaking my back all day trying to get the morning chores done. And I'm not going to feed again. They've had enough for one day. If I have to—"

"You have to," she said, her composure stiffening with annoyance at his overblown reaction.

"What?" His voice took on that I'm-the-boss tone.

"I'm not able to come home right now. You'll have to take care of the Rocking G for me. You said you could handle it. So, handle it."

"Billie—"

"Doug," she said, her voice stern, as if she were lecturing a child. "I don't know what happened to make the Jacobson kid quit. And I don't want to know. I'm trying to plan our wedding. Remember? I'm not having fun here, either." She altered the truth only slightly. Facing the fact that Nick didn't want her had become a crucifixion of her ego.

"This isn't a stress-free vacation," she continued, "where I'm sunning all day and having the time of my life. I'd much rather be where you are, mucking out stalls and doling out feed to a few docile animals than shopping for gifts and clothes and all this frilly girl stuff. So, handle it, as I'm handling my end of the bargain. Okay?''

''I'm not asking you to come home, Billie. I'm telling you.''

That comment felt like a spur along her spine. ''Doug, you will take care of the ranch. If you don't, then you're going to pay a hefty price for any damage done. You said any kid could handle it. So, prove it. Okay?''

Silence was his final comment. It burned her ears and ended when he disconnected the call. Her anger spewed out like a fire doused by a bucket of water. Doubts and uneasiness swirled inside her thoughts, muddled her thinking. Maybe she should go back. The ranch was her responsibility. She couldn't just turn her back on it. Did she really trust Doug to handle things?

And what the heck was she doing here? With Nick? Playing some kind of game that could never end with anything but heartache? Her heartache.

''What was that all about?'' Nick asked, startling her.

She turned and saw him in the doorway. A frown slanted his brows toward his straight nose. His hand remained on the door handle, tense, prepared for action. Behind him, Buddy bounded inside and ran toward her. The big furry beast rubbed his head against her knee and licked her hand. Managing a smile that was more shaky and tremulous than confident, she scratched behind the dog's ear, and his tail thumped against the floor.

''Doug.'' Aware of her damp top, she crossed her arms over her chest. ''He had a few problems at the ranch today.''

A smile tugged on Nick's mouth, loosening the worry from his dark eyes. ''Wait.'' He straddled a chair at the kitchen table and propped his arms along the back. ''This has got to be good.''

She bit back her own grin as an image of Doug carrying a bucket of feed into a bull pen and sidestepping cow patties popped into her mind. Trying not to encourage Nick's obvious amusement at her fiancé's trials, trying even harder to maintain her loyalty to Doug, she recounted the phone conversation, skimming over the misunderstanding.

Nick didn't laugh as she'd anticipated. He nodded, his mouth a straight line. "You did good. You did the right thing."

"I'm not so sure anymore. I spoke out of anger. He really scared me with talk of an emergency." Her hands still trembled, and she clasped them together. "I thought it was Mother. That something—"

"I know." His voice sounded deep and rich and soothing, calming her fears. He came toward her, wrapped a comforting arm around her shoulders. It made her want to lean into him, hold on to him. She'd lost so much. She didn't want to lose him, too. But how could she hang on to what she had no right to?

His warmth made her too aware of him, and far too cognizant of the reason she'd told Doug she wouldn't return so soon. Plain and simple, it was Nick.

His thumb made a small circle along her shoulder. Nothing in the gesture could have been called sensual. But it electrified her nerve endings and made her stomach drop. She wanted to turn into his embrace, but she didn't dare.

"I don't know what I'd do if something happened..." She absorbed his strength, breathed in his masculine scent of earth and wind. He derailed her train of thought. With laser-like precision, she focused on her mom, what it would be like to lose her last living relative. It got her mind off Nick. It made her throat shut down. "I've lost so much already."

It made her think. Made her think hard about what she was giving up. Maybe she was stupid to leave the ranch. What would happen to her mother there all alone?

"Hey." He squeezed her shoulder. "It's okay now. Your mom's fine. If there was any doubt, then I'd be the first one headed for Bonnet. You did the right thing, Billie. Doug's got to learn—"

"But what if there really is an emergency? Will he know how to handle it? Will he? What if he doesn't feed the cattle and horses properly. It's a lot of work. We should know."

"And Doug will know soon enough."

"I don't want the livestock to suffer because of my selfishness."

His jaw squared, the muscles clenching beneath the taut, tanned skin. "You're not selfish. You're the most unselfish person I know."

"You're wrong, Nick. I am selfish. And this won't be the last of troubles with ranch help. After the wedding, I'm enrolling in college. I'm going to be a vet."

Surprise made his hand tighten on her shoulder in an encouraging clasp. He flashed her a grin. "You should. You deserve it."

She shrugged her shoulders. "I don't know about that. But I worry about the ranch. Will we be able to find someone to handle things? Or will I start school and not be able to finish because some hired hand up and quits? And maybe what I'm doing is just ending up hurting the livestock. The horses and cattle are my responsibility. Mine. I feel like I'm disappointing my father."

"Hey." Nick grasped both of her shoulders and turned her to face him. He stared down at her, his eyes laser points aimed at her. "You've given up your whole life, your dreams, your ambitions to take care of that ranch. I'm proud of you, proud you're gutsy enough to go after your dreams." She dropped her gaze. He folded his hand along the side of her neck and with his thumb forced her chin up, until she met his liquid gaze. "Don't let go of them now, hold on." His voice held an urgency, insistence.

"The ranch can survive without you for one week, Billie. And longer when you start school. You'll find someone older and more stable than a high school kid. I'll help, if you need it. So don't worry. We'll figure this out."

She wanted to believe him, desperately wanted to hold on to his words like a lifeline. This time, she wanted to let him help her, like she wouldn't let him help her before.

"The livestock's not suffering. But Schaeffer..." He grinned, a broad smile that made his eyes sparkle with that old mischief she so easily recognized, that made her heart trip over itself. "Now he's the one suffering. Won't hurt him. And it might help you."

"I know, I know. He'll gain respect for what I've done these past years by myself."

Nick nodded. "That's right." He pulled her against him, held her against his chest and hooked his hands at the small of her back. He rested his cheek on the top of her head. Billie's pulse ricocheted through her body like the silver ball in a pinball machine. "Besides, you've got plans. While he's scooping oats and shoveling manure, we'll be dining on a simmering strip of prime rib."

He released her as suddenly as he'd pulled her against him, leaving her confused and wanting more. "Go on," he said, "get changed. We have reservations for seven o'clock."

It was a suit-and-tie establishment. Billie fit in easily wearing the dramatic black dress they'd bought the day before. It embraced her long, lithe form, stretching along each dip, each slope, each flaring curve like a rich, dark fudge flowing over butterscotch skin. It melted his resolve inch by inch. How could he resist this much temptation? He wanted to take a nibble of her narrow shoulder, taste her warm skin, breathe in that new delicious scent that reminded him of a moonlight evening, full of mystery and passion. His mouth watered for another kiss, another embrace...something more...something richer. He had a craving that could only be satisfied by Billie.

He remembered the words Billie had said to Doug on the phone earlier. He'd opened the kitchen door and heard her simple comment which had socked him in the gut like an iron fist. *My end of the bargain.*

Bargain? Is that what her marriage was? Had Billie struck some kind of a deal with her fiancé? Did they have an arranged marriage? A so-called marriage of convenience? Why would she do such a thing? Why would she give her life away like that...to a man like Schaeffer? Just so she could go to college? It seemed inconceivable. But he knew with Billie, she wasn't one to let life trample on her dreams.

It should have made him boiling mad. But it didn't. In fact, the scenario pleased him. Because it meant she wasn't in love with Doug Schaeffer. It meant she might be able to fall for Nick...again.

Another wallop to his gut knocked out his elation. A nest of squiggly worms entered his stomach, turning his insides out. The thought of Billie in love with him had him contemplating whether he could be in love with her. And that scared the stuffing out of him.

Tugging on his tie, he ordered another Scotch from the bartender while Billie sipped her Chardonnay. Soft, sensuous music wafted through the bar area while they waited for their table. He tried to ignore how the stardust lighting highlighted the straight line of her shoulder, the shimmer of her honey-gold tan. As she turned this way and that, looking the place over, he caught a glimpse of finely tuned muscles along her back. He tried to remember what the lady at the dress shop had called the opening framing a wide expanse from her shoulder blades to the dip in the small of her back. To him, it was far too big for a "keyhole," and far too sexy for his own good.

"Nice place," she said, her voice a little husky, a little too provocative.

Her glittering gaze scanned the burgundy leather seats, the polished floor, the sparkling glasses hanging upside down around the bar. She seemed to like the impeccable service, which made him feel crowded, like someone was always watching and waiting. Elegant diners sifted in and out of the area, looking as dazzling as the decor with luxuriant clothes of silk and satin and enough diamonds and pearls to start a jewelry store. He'd chosen this restaurant because it was considered the best, because Billie deserved the best. But it didn't impress him. It only reminded him of his ex-wife's incessant demands that he could never seem to reach.

"Do you come here often?" Billie asked.

"No." *Never*.

"Did you before? With Diane?" she asked, a strange tone making her voice crack. He wondered if Billie had the same expectations. After all, she'd been wined and dined by Schaeffer.

"I've never been here before," he confessed, feeling more like a fish out of water. Was it because of the restaurant? Or because of Billie? Not liking the way his second question made beads of sweat form along his back, he preferred to think the elegant restaurant made him feel inadequate. He could accept that. Diane had made him feel the same way. But it pained him to think he might disappoint Billie.

"Why tonight?" she asked, her eyes opening like deep blue pools swallowing him whole and somehow making him feel at home.

The muscles along his throat tightened. "I wanted it to be special. You deserve the best, Billie." Not a second-rate husband and third-class marriage with Schaeffer. "This is supposed to be the best. It's got a five-star rating. Don't ever settle for less."

Her eyes sparkled like sapphires. "I gather five's good?"

"We've got to get you off the ranch more often," he said with a smile. He wanted to offer her the same possibilities that Schaeffer could. But how? Would she accept anything from him?

A few minutes later they were seated in a cozy corner of the restaurant. A potted palm with its branches forming giant fans behind his chair gave them more seclusion from the other diners. He wondered if it was wise for him to be so isolated with Billie, as if they were marooned on a deserted island together. But then reality intruded. They weren't alone. The waiter brought the wine list in a leatherbound folder and handed it to Nick.

While Nick felt the pressure along his shoulders double, Billie eyed the silver bowl of bread placed in the center of the table along with sculpted pats of butter that looked like delicate yellow rosebuds. "I've never been to such an expensive place. I hope I don't spill something." She rubbed her fingers along the white linen tablecloth. "Or worse."

"You'll be fine," he said, but he wasn't so sure about himself.

His gaze scanned the pages and pages of red and white wines listed. Guessing from the spellings, most were French or Italian. All were difficult to pronounce, if not impossible. He could handle merlot or Chardonnay or even a Zinfandel. But it was never that simple. Which merlot? Which Cabernet? What the heck was "ri-o-jay"? He was sure his Texas accent would only make his pronunciation worse.

Then he glanced at the prices, did a double take and nearly choked on his Scotch. How could grape juice cost so much? Would it be too ill-bred to simply order a beer? No, no, he couldn't do that. He'd told Billie she deserved the best. And he'd show her. Did that mean he should order the most expensive wine? Because it dipped deeper into his wallet, was that proof it would be better than the rest?

What was he going to do? Point and order?

He remembered the humiliation of ordering in front of his ex-wife. With her green eyes flashing, she'd scorned his attempts. She'd given him a dozen books on selecting appropriate wines, none of which he'd ever opened. Finally, disgusted with his so-called "redneck" ways, she'd taken the responsibility from him and ordered wine at a dinner party with a flourish and a biting comment about his Texas vernacular disability. Their guests had laughed at her cutting remarks; Nick had realized then his marriage was coming to an end.

With crystal-clear memory, he also remembered taking Schaeffer and Billie to dinner in Bonnet. He'd offered to let Schaeffer choose the wine for dinner, not because he was such a gracious host, but because he hadn't wanted to make a fool of himself in front of Billie or her so-called fiancé. His thoughts jumbled together as he tried to piece back together the ritual Schaeffer had performed when the wine had been delivered to their table. His stomach sunk with a sick feeling of dread and regret. Now he'd probably embarrass Billie.

He'd brought her here to show her what she deserved, to wine and dine her, to treat her as a woman should be treated. A part of him wanted to impress her, show her that he could outclass Schaeffer. Okay, he revised that, not a part of him…all of him. He wanted to prove he was better than her fiancé. But was he?

"Would you like a bottle of wine this evening, sir?" the waiter, with his starched shirt and black bow tie, asked in a stiff, cordial manner.

A cold draft of apprehension blew over him. It was now or never. Slowly, he closed the wine list. "Billie, thirsty for anything in particular?"

Her eyes widened momentarily, then she tipped her chin down, deferring to his better or worse judgment, whichever it would prove to be.

"What do you recommend as your finest red?" he asked the waiter.

The older gentleman cocked his head to the side and studied Nick. He felt as if he somehow didn't measure up to the qualifications of the restaurant's finer guests. Mentally, Nick deducted a percentage from the waiter's tip. "Ah, well—" the waiter took the wine list from Nick "—the list is quite vast."

"It'd take me a year to single something out of here," Nick answered.

The waiter nodded. "Do you like a full-bodied wine or a lighter one?"

Frankly, he preferred plain ol' American-brewed beer, not the fancy English or German varieties. Just beer. Not heavy, not light. Regular, every day, ice-cold beer. Hoping for a safe answer, he said, "Medium."

"Oaky?" the waiter asked.

Dokey? Nick doubted that was the correct answer. He felt Billie's gaze on him. His shirt collar seemed to shrink as if he was boiling in hot water. "Yes," he ventured.

"Tannic?"

That threw him a double curve. He rubbed his jaw, not having a clue.

"Or do you prefer a fruitier blend?"

"Definitely not," he answered. Out of the corner of his eye, he saw Billie duck her head and hide a smile behind her hand. His insides burned. He wanted to crawl under the table, or better yet, toss in his white napkin of surrender and go somewhere else, someplace less pretentious, someplace that felt more like him.

Contemplating Nick's answers, the waiter tapped his chin. "Maybe a nice Pinot Noir." He twirled his tongue around several French-sounding names that left Nick's brain in a fog of uncertainty.

"What did you say first?" Nick arched a speculative brow. His skin felt hot as a drill bit when the frosty-haired waiter repeated the name of the wine. "That'll do."

"A wise selection," the waiter said with a slight bow as he backed away from their table.

Once again alone with his date—his Billie—he shifted his gaze toward her, dreading her laughter, her scorn, her embarrassment. Lines as delicate as cobwebs fanned out from the corners of her vivid blue eyes when she smiled at him. His throat went dry.

"I'm impressed," she said, her bedroom voice husky and inviting.

"How so?"

"How'd you know all that about wine?"

He laughed, the sound bursting out of him. "I don't know anything. I just answered the guy's questions."

"Yeah, but you knew what you liked, what tan... tannenbaum...whatever—" she swiveled her wrist "—meant. And what's 'oaky'?"

"Hell, if I know." He shook his head. "I just knew I didn't want it fruity." His voice inflection made Billie laugh.

He joined her, the sounds of their laughter harmonizing. Both of them leaned forward, toward each other, until their gazes locked and held. Until something sizzled between them. A spark. A flash of insight.

Abruptly, they each sat back, sinking into their leather chairs. Nick shifted his gaze away from her. She fiddled with the napkin in her lap. He grabbed the menu off the table and hid behind it. This was dangerous. He wished he understood the explosive feelings building inside him. Then he might know if he should proceed or retreat.

"So, you're not a wine expert," she said, drawing his attention from the list of steaks.

"Wouldn't know an oaky if I met one."

Her full, throaty laugh escaped her. She tilted her head back, exposing her long, sleek neck. Her silky hair fell past her shoulders like a golden cascade. Nick wanted to lean across the table and kiss her, right on that pulse point at the base of her throat. When she looked at him again, her blue eyes seemed darker, like midnight, mysterious and intoxicating as a shot of bourbon.

Wanting, needing to get a grip on his attraction to Billie, he fisted the Scotch glass and tossed back the last of his drink. "Now if you want to know beer, I'm your man."

"Beer, huh?" She gave him a sultry smile that had steam rising off his skin. Her tongue darted out and licked her lips with longing. "Nothing better than a good cold one on a hot summer afternoon."

He'd never thought of drinking beer as sexy, but with Billie he had no doubts it would be. But not as much as putting his mouth on hers, drawing in the taste of her, feeling her soft and warm and willing in his arms. The ice cubes in his glass clinked together, chilling her effects on him briefly. But he knew it wouldn't take much to send him over the edge of wanting into pure need.

"Why don't we?" she asked, placing her napkin beside her plate.

"What?"

"Go. Get that ice-cold beer. Relax." She rolled her head from side to side as if easing the kinks in her neck. "This place makes me nervous. I feel like I've been on my best behavior as long as possible."

"What about dinner?"

"We haven't ordered. Cancel the wine and we'll be on our way." She lowered her voice. "I don't think either of us is comfortable here. So why stay? It's ridiculous. We can grab a burger somewhere. Somewhere that has good beer."

He smiled. This was his kind of woman—down to earth, able to see the humor in a situation, and sexy beyond comprehension. The kind he could definitely fall in love with.

Chapter Eight

That was the Nick Latham Billie remembered and loved. Part macho, I-know-everything male, part vulnerable little boy. Together he equaled the man who'd stolen her heart. And he took it again.

Sitting at a drive-in, parked beneath a white metal awning lined with pink and green neon lights, Billie ordered a double cheeseburger, extra-large French fries smothered in cheese and a quart-size beer. Who cared about calories when her heart was going to be broken soon?

Nick gave her a mischievous smile that had her stomach turning somersaults and placed the same order for himself, adding a side of onion rings. Instead of joining in the cholesterol bath, Doug would have given her a raised eyebrow and a hint that he expected her to retain her slim figure after the wedding.

Grateful for Nick's enthusiasm and similar tastes, she gave him a wry smile in return. "I'm on to you."

He'd removed his dinner jacket and had rolled up the sleeves of his starched white shirt. He lifted his hands off the leather steering wheel of his Jaguar. "What? What'd I do now?"

"I've figured out your new strategy for stopping my wedding." She was beginning to think there was one way he could stop it for good. But she doubted he'd give her his heart in exchange for breaking her promise to Doug. "You're going to fatten me up so I can't fit in my wedding gown, right?"

"That's it." He chuckled. "You're too smart for me."

She leaned back against the headrest and felt the soft, evening breeze drift over her like a lazy caress. Her skin puckered, and she wrapped her arms across her middle, enjoying the night, the smell of hot grease and cold brew, and being with an old, dear friend.

"You cold?" he asked, putting a hand on her arm, his fingers making her insides red-hot. "If so, I'll put the top up."

"No," she said, her voice crackling like soda poured over ice cubes. "It feels good. Makes me remember the good ol' days. When we used to camp out."

"I still have that orange pup tent we used. We could set it up in the backyard."

Her grin widened. She shifted in her seat and slipped off her high-heel pumps, wiggling her toes. "I don't know, sleeping on the ground doesn't sound as comfortable anymore."

"I agree. I'm getting too old for lying on the ground."

"My favorite part was in the chill of the morning, starting a campfire, and cooking bacon and eggs, then pan-frying toast."

"Nothing better," he agreed. "I liked night the best. Curling up in my sleeping bag, knowing you were on one side and Jake on the other...and that your folks were just a couple of feet away. It felt like what a family should be. What I didn't have at home.''

Her heart opened to him and her hand reached for his. ''Ah, Nick. I know it was hard when you lost your mom. But I had no idea how much you were missing at home.''

''I didn't miss much. Your family provided me with all the love and support I could stand. I almost looked forward to when Dad would travel and I'd have to come stay with y'all. I even liked singing those silly songs your mother taught us. And listening to those ghost stories your dad made up.''

''They used to scare me,'' she said, remembering seeing ghosts and goblins in the dark shadows.

''Not me. With your family, I never felt so safe.'' His features shifted and closed, as if he'd said too much, revealed a hidden piece of himself. ''Remember playing Monopoly late at night? Jake always had to be the boot.''

''And you had to be the race car.'' She went along with the ebb and flow of the conversation and didn't dwell on his yearnings as a young boy because it made her yearnings as a woman even stronger. ''And you always won. But I liked sneaking chips and salsa into our bedrooms and telling bad jokes,'' she said with a chuckle. She released his hand and gave him a slight punch in the shoulder. ''And you and Jake teaching me about strip poker.''

He gave her a smoldering look. ''We didn't really strip. Not everything. Besides, it was all in fun. We were young. It wasn't sexual.''

Maybe not then. But it sure would be now. ''Uh-huh. Dad didn't think so. Good thing he came upstairs when he did.''

Nick laughed, his shoulders shaking with the effort to suppress his humor. ''Jake and I had to muck out the stalls for a month for that one. But you weren't so innocent, either. What about that time you stole our clothes down at Willow's Pond?''

''Hey, I left your shoes!'' Her stomach cinched tight from laughing so hard. She twisted in her seat, facing him, enjoying the warm smile on his face, the easiness between them. ''Mom told you not to go skinny-dipping. Y'all did it anyway. But you wouldn't let me go. Y'all took off running when I wasn't looking and dodged me all afternoon. But I finally found you down at the pond. So I sneaked around the bushes till I'd picked up all your clothes off the bank. Y'all were too busy splashing and diving to notice li'l ol' me.''

She snickered, remembering the boys' shock, anger, then bloodred embarrassment. They'd wanted to run after her but their bravery shriveled in the cooler breeze of evening as they stood on the bank dripping wet. They'd slunk back into the water rather than chase after her naked as jaybirds. ''I thought Jake was gonna skin me alive.''

''I would have helped.'' His laughter dwindled. ''Did you ever know what happened after you ran back to the house?''

''No.'' Her eyes widened. ''What?''

''After the sun went behind the clouds, we started to get cold. That made us brave. Better to stalk back naked than freeze our butts off. So we climbed out of the pond. Right about then Marcie Dempster, Jean Chapman and Rayanne Burke came walking up.''

''Oh, no!'' Billie's eyes bulged. She flopped back against her seat, laughing.

He shook his head, the tips of his ears turning to scarlet. ''I don't know which of us was more shocked, the girls or me and Jake. But we dove back in the water and they took off runnin'." He managed a frown, but a smile lurked at the corners of his mouth. "So, Billie, thanks for one of the most embarrassing moments of my life."

Stifling her laughter only a little, she mused, "You're quite welcome. Glad I could be such a fond memory from your childhood."

He gave her a rueful grin.

"So, what was another embarrassing moment in the life of Nick Latham?" she asked, giving him a beguiling smile.

His grin faded. His eyes turned stone-cold. She'd struck a raw nerve. "Which one?" he asked, his voice crusty. "My ex-wife provided me with several. They're not as funny, though."

"Oh." Billie couldn't manage to say anything else. Suddenly her heart ached at the pain in his voice, the grief darkening his eyes. She wanted to reach out to him, but had she already tripped over an invisible line between them? Had she already said too much?

The roller-blading waitress brought their dinner and drinks. Nick paid the bill, then handed Billie's burger to her. They left both orders of fries in the sack and sat it between them for easy access. The sounds of the night—distant horns honking, a siren's wail, a giggling laugh from a nearby car—closed in on them as if insulating them from the outside world. They busied themselves with ketchup and biting into the thick, juicy burgers.

"We were so different," he said after a few minutes. "Diane and I. Sometimes I wonder how we ever got together."

The bag crinkled as Billie reached for a fry. She held her breath, wanting Nick to continue, wanting to get a closer glimpse of his heart.

He shrugged his left shoulder. "She was beautiful. Or

at least, I thought so. Beautiful on the outside. But on the inside…well, I figured that out later.''

Biting into his burger, he contemplated his thoughts before swallowing and continuing. ''So, okay, I admit, I was in lust, not love, when I married. I don't think I knew the difference then. But what did she ever see in me? I mean, from day one of our marriage, all she did was point out my faults. Made me wonder what good things she ever saw that made her want to marry me in the first place.''

''Oh, Nick.'' Her throat felt tight with anger and pain. ''You're handsome, sweet, attentive…funny, decisive, a leader. Any girl would fall for you.''

''Nah, it wasn't that. She saw potential, I guess. But she wanted to improve me, make me better, fix me.''

Billie winced inside. Wasn't that what she'd allowed Doug to start doing with her?

''Hell, I guess Diane was right. I do have a lot of faults. Too many. But the hard truth is, she loved what she thought I'd be. She loved my earning potential.''

''Your 'earning potential'?'' she asked, stuffing the last fry into her mouth and washing it down with a good swallow of beer.

''Yeah. Through college, I was being groomed to run my dad's company.'' He wadded up the waxed paper that had held his burger and dunked it in the paper sack like a two-point basket. ''I drove a slick car. A 'stud mobile,' as my friends called it. It impressed the girls. I had a great tan from working each summer and most weekends at one of Dad's construction sites. And I'd made good money. I bought her presents, took her to decent restaurants when other guys were going to burger joints and a movie for dates. But Diane saw the potential for me to make a mint. And she wanted part of that.''

He glanced at his wallet on the dash. "Well, she's got a part of it now." He turned toward Billie. The neon lights above them made the lines in his face seem harsher, deeper. He looked far older than the boy she'd known, wiser, more introspective, more reflective. "But the hard truth was, she hated that I worked with my hands. Hated that I got mud on my boots and dirt under my nails. She liked the fact I had my own business, but hated what that business was. I was her most embarrassing moment."

"Oh, Nick. How awful! How could she—"

"It wasn't all her fault. I was a disappointment."

"How? What did you do?"

"I couldn't please her. I didn't know what a woman wanted. How many times did she tell me that? I didn't know how to make her happy. Maybe it was because I didn't really grow up with a mom. Diane wasn't like any of the other girls I'd ever known."

A pain struck Billie in the heart like a pointed arrow. She'd been Nick's closest girl friend, a buddy. But she hadn't had the same needs or desires as a woman like Diane. She felt the unintentional barb slice through an old wound. She was a tomboy. She always would be. And Nick would always see her that way.

"One afternoon," he said, "I came home early, hoping to surprise my bride with tickets for a long weekend in sunny Mexico. We'd been having problems. I'd been working later and later, and I thought this would help us get closer, give us time together.

"I was wrong. As usual. She was having a tea party with all her high-falutin' friends. Wives of doctors and lawyers." He took a swig of his beer. "She met me at the back door. Asked me to stay outside till they all left. God, there was panic on her face. Like she might have to introduce me or something. And it was my damn house! I was being treated like a servant.''

"What did you do?" she asked, unable to see Nick hanging around outside his house waiting for a bunch of pretentious women to leave.

"I said to hell with her and stomped inside, trailing mud chunks behind me. The ladies stopped their conversations when I entered the living room. I didn't wait for Diane to introduce me. I told them I was her gardener. And the next day I filed for divorce."

"Oh, Nick." Her eyes welled up with tears. The pain and humiliation stung her. It burned in her soul, radiating anger and disbelief. How could anyone be embarrassed by Nick? How could anyone treat their husband with so little regard?

"See, Billie, marriage without respect can't work."

She knew what he was saying in a not-so-indirect way. She had flashes of Doug straightening her collar, giving her a disgruntled eye if she used the wrong fork at dinner, cutting her off midsentence if she brought up an inappropriate topic with clients. Doug had worried she'd embarrass him. Would he treat her like Diane had treated Nick?

A more recent memory popped to the surface and warmed her from the inside out. She remembered Nick hurrying her to the trailer, avoiding the crew, snapping at Jody who'd flirted with her. He'd worried she'd attract a flock of men!

She looked at him then, his proud forehead, his strong jaw, his intense tiger eyes boring into her. With him, she felt protected and wildly excited. Putting her fears of rejection behind her, she placed a hand against his warm cheek, feeling the rough beard beneath her palm, sensitizing her nerve endings. She curled her fingers around the edge of his jaw and brought his face to hers.

Her mouth opened against his, hot, moist, eager. She loved this man, loved his strength, his vulnerability, his humanity. Although he didn't know it, he'd experienced with his wife what she'd always felt—inadequate, insecure, rebellious. She wanted him to know she understood his heartbreak, embarrassment and anger. But words couldn't convey her meaning. So she put her heart and soul into a sizzling kiss that had her opening her heart and body to him.

This time, as she planted a kiss on him with a little more expertise than she'd had as a teenager, she felt him respond and kiss her back, fully, completely. Her world tilted upside down. Her body came alive in his arms, pulsating, throbbing, yearning for more, much more.

He kissed her mouth, the sensitive flesh along the underside of her jaw, the length of her throat. Her pulse jolted at the warm contact of his lips nipping at her flesh. Her breath snagged on a moan. His name caught in her throat.

"Billie," Nick mumbled against her mouth. "My sweet Billie." His palm found her breast and massaged it, sending hot pulses coursing through her body as she arched her back toward him.

"Oh, Nick. Don't stop...please..."

He captured her chin between thumb and forefinger and forced her to look into his glowing eyes, which reminded her of melted copper. "Don't marry Schaeffer, Billie. Please, for God's sake, don't marry him."

She wanted to say, "Okay, yes, whatever you want." But she swallowed the words that would be her undoing. From somewhere deep inside she found the strength to straighten her spine, to resist Nick. She wanted a reason—a good reason, something other than his big brother satisfaction or jealousy or hatred of Doug Schaeffer. She wanted Nick to want her, need her, as much as she needed and wanted him.

"Why?" Her voice cracked, and she tried again, her need stronger than her fear. "Why, Nick?"

He stared into her anguish-filled eyes. He knew the answer she wanted. Each beat of his heart answered her question.

Billie, his Billie, wanted everything from him, more than he could possibly give. His confidence with women had, like cat claws through fabric, been shredded. Tattered. Ripped. He'd had a woman want him for money. Could Billie ever want him for himself? Could she love him? How would he ever know? If she was so desperate to settle for Schaeffer, then she might settle for Nick without love. He couldn't accept that. His heart rolled in on itself into a tight ball of doubt and regret.

He loved Billie too much to— *He loved Billie.*

The thought struck him hard. Stumbling back from the impact, he questioned himself. Could that be true? Did he love Billie? Love her like a man should love a woman?

Of course, he loved her. He pushed back the panic rising inside him with that truth. He loved her, not just as a little sister, but as a friend.

She was a friend. A friend. That was all. Wasn't it?

They'd grown up together, shared so many memories and suffered insurmountable losses. But those losses had somehow brought them together, gave them an understanding for each other, deepened their love. Could his love be deeper than friendship?

For many years he'd depended on both her and Jake to be the family he'd lost, to make him smile once again.

But with Jake's death, had they lost the one link keeping them close—Jake himself? Had he lost Billie's friendship in the years they'd spent apart? And in that, had he lost a piece of himself?

Or maybe he simply didn't know Billie as he once had. Maybe that missing piece opened his eyes to new possibilities. Or more likely, showed him that he meant less to her than he'd believed, hoped and now missed. Was he simply trying to recover a missing piece of himself?

Strong, resourceful and independent, Billie Rae Gunther didn't need him as he needed her. She didn't need anyone. Hadn't she told him that when he'd offered to help her with the ranch after Jake's death? It stung like a barb in his side. She'd rejected his offer; she'd rejected him. So maybe the love he felt for her was simply a longing for the past and all they'd shared and meant to each other. He was clinging to the past and all he'd recently lost, when she was embracing the future.

"Why don't you want me to marry Doug?" Billie interrupted his thoughts with her point-blank question, her tone harsher than before, as if she'd shielded herself from disappointment.

Struggling with the reasons buried deep in his heart and the confusion in his brain, he used the most obvious argument available. "Because you're not in love with Schaeffer."

"I never said I was." Bold and brave as the blue in the American flag, her eyes met his. She lifted her chin with a proud tilt of her head. "But there are other valid reasons for marriage. Love isn't always the best."

"It helps."

"And it hurts." She looked so damn beautiful, so valiant with her squared shoulders, graceful neck, challenging lift of her chin. She was a worthy opponent and partner. But not for Doug Schaeffer. But was she perfect for Nick?

"I don't know what's going on in that head of yours..." He tapped his finger against her temple. "But I'm guessing you want to get married for money, to ease the burden of the ranch, to pursue your degree. But, Billie—"

"Don't, Nick." A tick throbbed in her jawline, right beneath the surface of her delicate skin. "You don't know the struggles I've been through. You don't know the financial straits Jake left the ranch in, the debt..." She paused for a moment as if getting her emotions back under control. "I'm not going to talk about this with you. You can't understand."

When she turned away from him to stare resolutely out the passenger window, he grabbed her elbow and made her face him again. "I don't care what your reasons were. My question is, what's Schaeffer getting out of all of this? What's his reason for marrying you?"

A tiny flicker in the depths of her eyes told him he'd wounded her with his carelessly aimed question. Again. It reiterated that he had no business trying to love Billie. He'd only end up hurting her. And he couldn't endure that.

She arched a narrow brow at him in derision. "I know it's impossible for you to imagine that anyone could find me attractive, that anyone could fall in love with me. But I'm a flesh-and-blood woman beneath my jeans and boots." She glanced down at the black sheath dress she wore. "It's not always obvious to others, but there's a woman in here." She pressed her hand against her chest. "With real needs and desires."

The fire in her eyes sparked a flame inside him—a

greedy blaze of inextinguishable desire—that would burn forever.

"Maybe, just maybe, Doug is capable of seeing that," she said, her hands curling into fists. "Maybe he doesn't love me any more than I love him. So what? Many throughout history didn't wait for a love match, and they survived, their marriages flourished. Love can grow. If you give it the opportunity. If you give it room."

She took a shaky breath and opened her hands, palms down along her thighs, her fingers stretching, reaching for some invisible quest. She toyed with the diamond on her ring finger, rolling it around and around. The intricate cuts in the stone caught the reflection of the neon lights.

A dreadful heaviness filled Nick.

"I didn't mean you weren't a woman, that you weren't desirable," Nick said. "I just wondered if Schaeffer will be happy with a vet for a wife."

"Why not?" she snapped. "What's wrong with a vet? Or a tomboy?"

He hadn't intended to insult her with his twisted words. Cursing himself, he tried again. "I wouldn't want you to get in a situation like I was in with Diane."

"I appreciate your concern, but I'm not your responsibility. You don't have to worry about me."

"I know that. You're a strong, capable woman, Billie. I'm proud of what you've done with the ranch. I have no doubts you'll be a wonderful vet. But I can't help worrying about you."

"I know, I know," she said, hurt and anger mingling in her husky voice. "You're my big brother, standing in for Jake and all that foolishness.

"Doug and I respect each other," she said, her voice as quiet as his heartbeat was loud in his ears. "After this week—" her mouth quirked in a phantomlike smile

"—he'll respect me even more. We'll make a good team. I'll be the kind of wife a president of a company needs. He'll support me through school."

The hair at the back his neck stood erect. So it was for money. He could give her that. Then, when he'd sorted through his feelings, when she'd had a chance to know him again, maybe something could develop. Maybe. "I can't see Doug wanting a vet for his perfect company wife."

"What's wrong with what I want to do?"

"Nothing. You'll be wonderful. But I don't think you know Doug very well. If it's just a matter of money, I could help you—"

"I don't need *your* money. Don't you see, it's more than that? So much more. Doug and I will be partners in life. Money can't provide that." She drew a sure, confident breath.

Silenced by her heartfelt words—how he'd managed to wound her when he hadn't meant to—Nick started to see things differently. Maybe Billie knew what she was getting herself into. Love had been lacking from his marriage, but more importantly, so had been respect. The memories left a bitter taste in his mouth. His bruised confidence from his divorce and Billie's passionate defense of Schaeffer made him think maybe she could make a go of a marriage grounded in respect. No matter how much it tormented him, maybe he should take a step back, and let Billie marry Schaeffer without any interference.

"Nick?" She broke into his thoughts with a butter-soft whisper. "Why'd you kiss me tonight? Was it just another experiment?"

He detected a slight waver in her voice. "You kissed me, remember?"

"So that's all it was. You responded to me…out of pity, obligation, what?" Her voice hit a shrill note that skewered his heart as she searched for a reason he couldn't give.

Without thinking of the consequences or the impropriety, knowing she might slap him or at the least push him away, he grabbed her shoulders and hauled her against him. He read hesitation and anguish in her eyes. But not fear, never fear. That would have stopped him cold.

Slanting his mouth over hers, he kissed her, devouring and invading with his tongue. Silencing her damn questions and his self-doubt, he stole her breath, as well, taking her essence inside him, savoring the scent and flavor of her. She was a part of him. She always would be.

But he had to let her go.

Using superhuman strength, he released her. He curled his fingers over the steering wheel and slanted a glance in her direction. Her mouth looked dewy, her eyes misty. She blinked, her breathing unsteady. "Does that answer your question? I'm attracted to you," he growled, his chest heaving with the effort of breathing. "Okay? You're a beautiful woman. Don't ever doubt that. Schaeffer ought to be shot for giving you doubts."

"He didn't," she said, her voice breathy.

His gaze met hers, questioning her statement.

She swallowed hard. "You did, Nick. A long time ago."

He cursed himself. Her words crushed him. His ex-wife had been right. He didn't know how to treat a woman. He wouldn't risk hurting Billie again. His knuckles turned white against the supple leather steering wheel. "Then I should be shot for not making you feel beautiful, desirable, sexy."

He released the steering wheel and raked his fingers through his hair. "Don't you see? I l—" He broke off, catching himself before he committed a worse sin. "I care about you so much."

If only she knew. If only she knew what was in my heart. What I can't face.

"But I'm not the marrying kind." He forced the words out. "I've been down that one-way aisle. It's a long way back alone. I've learned my lesson about marriage." His throat tightened, choking the words that he wanted to say to her and constricting the words that would rip out his own heart.

"I prefer a loveless union," Billie stated, having turned away from him, her arms crossed over her stomach, her expression determined. "Love is too painful, too uncertain."

He looked straight through the windshield. He couldn't look at Billie and get the words out, the words that needed to be said. "If you want to marry Schaeffer, Billie, then I'll support you. I'll always be there when you need me. And if you want, if it's what *you* want, not what your mother wants, then I'll walk you down the aisle and give you away."

But he thought that might kill him.

Chapter Nine

Give her away? Nick wanted to give her away!

Billie could have kicked the slats out of the four-poster bed then tossed the whole thing, mattress, springs and frame, out the second-story window. Hands clenched, breathing shallow, she paced the length of the bed in the room Nick had let her use in his great, big, oversize house. One story below, he was getting ready for bed, oblivious of the state he'd left her in. With each clipped step muffled by the plush carpet, Billie's anger went up a degree until her blood sizzled in her veins.

Her knees gave way, and she sunk onto the bed. She couldn't let him give her away to Doug, to anyone. She wasn't a possession to be bartered or sold. She was a woman with dreams and desires. And those still centered around Nick.

How could the one man she'd ever loved—still loved—want to give her away? How could she let him? How could she stand at the front of the church and pledge her love to another man? When her heart would always belong to Nicholas Barrett Latham.

As the night wore on and tears stabbed the backs of her eyes, she grabbed her suitcase, jerked open the brass locks and shoved up the lid with a determination born of desperation. She couldn't stay here. She had to leave. A pile of clothes formed at the bottom of the suitcase as she carelessly tossed in the oversize T-shirt she usually slept in, her toothbrush, the dresses she'd bought. Slamming the lid down on the jumble of clothes, she looked at the one article she'd purposefully left out.

She ran her fingers over the soft, gauzy material, lifted the nightgown and breathed in the scent of the cologne she'd purchased along with it. It had been a foolish purchase. This had been an even more foolish trip. Why had she ever thought she could prove Nick no longer had a hold on her heart? She'd proved the exact opposite. And now she'd have to live with the consequences for the rest of her life.

In that lingerie store she'd reacted to Nick's heated stare like a lovesick teenager. But not anymore. He'd made his intentions perfectly clear. He didn't want marriage. He didn't want her. The reality of it chewed through her heart like a vicious coyote on a hunt, tearing apart her confidence, ripping to shreds her dreams.

She'd fed Nick some line about wanting Doug's respect. But honestly, she wanted Nick's. Her hand curled into the soft fabric of the nightgown and made a tight fist. Tossing the gown across the room, she decided to leave it behind, with her lost desires.

She didn't want it. She didn't want Nick.

The lie struck her like a slap. But she ignored the sharp, stinging pain. She'd go on lying to herself, saying she didn't love Nick, until someday she believed it.

She grabbed her suitcase and purse, tiptoed down the stairs and called herself a cab. She'd marry Doug Schaeffer. He was her best choice for a groom. At least *he* wanted her, for whatever reason.

"Go on." He nudged the shaggy dog. "Go wake up Billie."

Buddy barked, then turned and trotted up the stairs toward the guest room. After a restless night where, in between long, cold showers, Nick had tossed and turned like a ship navigating hurricane-tossed waters, the memory of her kiss crashed over him like a tidal wave. The words they'd spoken last night churned and swelled in his head.

He'd decided to let Billie sleep late, thinking she deserved the rest, but it was almost nine. Was she sick? Billie was usually up before God. Unable to wait any longer, Nick had to get to the office. Jody had called with an interesting start to the day. Doug Schaeffer was waiting at the office to talk with Nick. Now what did Billie's groom want? Nick had considered leaving Billie a note, but he wanted to make sure she was okay, that what they'd shared and said last night hadn't severed their friendship for good.

A few minutes later Buddy's nails clicked against the wooden stairs. Nick turned away from the sun spilling through the bank of windows and frowned at his dog. "What'd you do? I said to get Billie, not her clothes."

He pulled the gauzy nightgown out of Buddy's mouth, the tags still dangling from the armhole. Just what he needed, a sexy reminder of Billie. Turning the soft-as-skin material over in his hands, he remembered the vulnerable, little-girl look in her eyes as she'd fit the loose fabric over her own curves. That same look had slowly turned like the tide, into a bold, hot stare, reflecting his own wants, needs and desires.

Touching this gown felt as luxuriant as sifting his fingers through Billie's silky blond hair or skimming his fingers along her butter-soft skin. He'd told her last night that he wasn't the marrying kind, and he wasn't. Billie deserved only the best. That excluded Schaeffer...and Nick. After a night of sorting through his confusing emotions, he knew his attraction to her was real, too real. But he wouldn't risk hurting Billie. And he knew if he pursued her, he'd hurt her.

Crumpling the gown in his hand, he tossed it onto the coffee table and headed upstairs. He couldn't think of her in that way anymore. He had to stop. He had to quit her like a bad habit.

"Billie," he called. "I'm going to work. If you want breakfast, there's..." His words drifted into nothing.

The silence and emptiness of the bedroom closed in around Nick. Questions churned inside his brain. He jerked open the guest bedroom closet. A lone hanger hung from the rack. Her suitcase and clothes were gone. The only thing left was that damn nightgown. Left to torture him with what should never be.

As if she'd spray-painted the wall with a goodbye note, he knew she'd returned home...to Schaeffer...to get married.

A crack opened his heart. He imagined her walking down the church aisle without him...toward her groom. A groom that wasn't him. A picture of her kissing Doug, leaning into him, her hand upon his heart, seared Nick's brain. Like a roll of film sliding past his vision, he saw snapshots of her future—dinner with executives, schoolwork, a veterinary clinic opening, and babies...little towheaded babies that had Billie's pert nose and her wide blue eyes. Schaeffer's babies. Nick's heart caved in on itself.

He wanted Billie's babies to be his, wanted her to belong to him in a till-death-do-us-part kind of way. Finally, after all this time, after hours of struggling and fighting his feelings, he faced facts. He loved Billie…not as a sister…more than a friend. He wanted her as his wife.

But he couldn't have her. Not if she wanted to marry someone else…someone like Doug Schaeffer…for whatever reason. The realization sliced through his heart like a razor blade through butter. At first painless, almost shocking, then as his love began to flow like blood from a wound, the searing pain took hold.

How could he love her, as she deserved to be? He understood her, anticipated her needs less than he had his ex-wife. If he'd failed there, wouldn't he fail with Billie? And she would mean more…so much more.

"Billie? Billie Rae?"

She felt a hand on her shoulder and forced her heavy eyelids open. Wanting to pull the pillow over her head, she pushed herself to sit up and greet her mother.

"What are you doing home so soon? When did you get here? The middle of the night?" Martha Gunther's blue eyes showed deep motherly concern. She tightened the sash of her wine-colored robe that made her disheveled hair look like silver moonbeams. "Are you sick?" Her cool hand cupped Billie's cheek.

"No, Mom," she mumbled, but she felt like she had a case of the flu. Her body ached. Her head throbbed. Her heart felt as if a spike had pierced it. "I'm fine."

She rubbed the sleep out of her eyes and swung her feet over the edge of the sofa. It had still been dark when she'd arrived home in the early morning hours. Her eyes grainy, her body bone-weary, she'd let herself into the ranch house and curled up on the sofa for a short nap before dawn, before she started in on the chores at the barn. From the slant of the light coming through the cracks in the drapes, she guessed she'd overslept.

"You don't look fine," her mother said, her brow wrinkling with the I-know-you-better-than-that frown. "You look like hell."

Surprised by her mother's language, *her* mother who never said anything dirtier than "spit," Billie slanted a gaze up at her. "Thanks a lot. Good to see you, too."

"Oh, sugar, I missed you." Planting a kiss on the top of her daughter's head, Martha moved toward the kitchen. "Why don't I fix a pot of coffee and we can discuss what happened?"

What happened? Billie sat up straighter, her skin prickling with heat. Instantly she thought of Nick's kiss, the sweet, thorough caress of his mouth against hers, the touch of his warm hand on her breast. Even now, hours later, in the cool morning hours, her body responded to the memory as if he'd just touched her. Her skin tightened. Her insides dissolved with a hot, aching need. Placing her fingers against her lips, she could still feel the urgent pressure, the branding heat, the delicious taste of him.

"What do you mean?" she asked tentatively, worried her mother could see some sort of evidence that she'd kissed Nick.

"Didn't you have a lover's quarrel?" Martha plopped the coffee filter into the maker.

Billie blinked. Did everyone know how she felt about Nick? "I—I guess." More one-sided, though. She shoved her fingers through her tangled hair. "I mean…

no, not really." She shook her head. It couldn't be considered a lover's quarrel when they weren't lovers, could it? They would *never* be lovers. The thought twisted the spike further into her heart.

"Sure seemed that way," her mother mused, measuring out the right amount of coffee grounds. "Doug slammed the phone down and barreled out of here yesterday, cursing a blue streak and—"

"Doug?" Billie asked, then understood. Relief rolled through her, but in the trail it left behind, guilt settled like fine dust.

"What's going on here?" A deep male voice gave Billie's heart a jolt. She swiveled toward the hallway that led to her mother's bedroom. "What's all the racket?" the voice repeated. "Where'd you go, sugar dumplin'?"

"M-Mom?" Billie stuttered, shock sending ice cubes through her veins. "Mr. Jacobson? Harold Jacobson and my...my m-m-mother!"

Her gaze flickered between the two middle-aged adults wearing bathrobes and slippers as if they were visiting Hugh Hefner's mansion. It didn't slip past Billie's attention that Harold Jacobson, her neighbor, and once her Ag teacher, was wearing her father's familiar, blue plaid robe. Her temper flared.

"What's—" She stood and braced her hands on her hips. "What's going on here? Why are you in my daddy's robe? Mother, why is a man walking out of your bedroom wearing Daddy's robe?"

"Oh, sugar." Martha came around the kitchen counter toward her daughter, her blue eyes troubled. "Forgive us for being so indelicate about this." She waved Harold away with a flick of her wrist. "Harry, go on and get dressed while I have a moment with my daughter." She had the good graces to blush at the awkward predicament.

Sniffing loudly and clearing his throat, Harold Jacobson mumbled, "Mornin', Billie Rae." He turned around and shuffled back down the hall toward her mother's bedroom.

Arching a brow, Billie faced her mother. She felt unbalanced, as if she'd been hobbled like a horse. "Forget to tell me something?"

"No, honey, I just... Well, there wasn't anything to tell...until last night." At this confession her mother's cheeks blazed, making her eyes look brilliant in the morning light. "You see, after Doug left yesterday, I was all worried about the ranch." She wrung her hands like one of her favorite dish towels. "I called Harold. You know your father and Harold were ranching buddies. And he's always been a help when we needed advice since your daddy's been gone. He came straight over. I was worried about you and the ranch and the wedding... everything and...well...."

"And a trip to the barn ended in your bedroom?" she asked, shock making her thoughts trip over themselves.

Martha crossed her arms over her chest. "I don't appreciate your tone, young lady. I'm a grown woman with needs. I've been a widow for five long years. I don't owe you or anyone else an explanation for my actions."

Having heard almost the same words out of her own mouth not twenty-four hours ago, she felt a smile tug at her lips. "Sorry, Mom. It's just...you surprised me, is all. Give me a minute to catch up."

"Oh, Billie, you know I loved your father more than anything. I grieved him something awful. I still do. Nobody could ever replace him in my heart. But that doesn't mean I don't have room to love another.

"Then your brother died. There's nothing harder than losing a child. Even though Jake was a man, it's not something you ever prepare yourself for. A parent, yes. A spouse, maybe, if you live long enough. But a child…'' She blinked back tears. ''When Harry's wife died, we understood the losses we'd both suffered. I started having these urges, these needs.''

Billie's gaze flicked back to where Harold Jacobson had been standing a moment earlier. ''So how did—'' she waggled her finger ''—*this* happen?''

''Well, we never made it to the barn.'' The corners of her mouth pinched her cheeks into an embarrassed smile. ''Oh, you know about that sort of thing, I'm sure. After all, you're an engaged woman. You know what love can do to you.''

Love? Billie almost choked on the word. Her mind had gone numb after her mother said it.

''We started talking about parenting worries.'' She patted Billie's arm. ''No matter how old you children get, we still worry, we still hurt for you. We talked about losing our spouses, the burden of taking care of a ranch, the sacrifices and struggles and…'' She shrugged as if that explained how she and Harold had ended up in bathrobes.

''Harry and I are in love,'' she stated. ''We've been playing that cat and mouse game for months, eyeing each other at church socials, in town at the grocery store, anywhere we happened to run into each other. And of course, every time he's been out to check on the ranch to see if you'd needed anything, he stayed around and had a cup of coffee with me.

''I must admit, it's a little different the second time around. I mean, we've both been married and widowed. We both know what we want in a mate. Once we knew the feeling was mutual then, well…'' She closed her hand over the opening of her robe at the base of her throat

as if she'd revealed too much of her own heart and longings.

"Don't you be thinking nothing bad about your
mother, Billie Rae." Hair combed into place, Harold
reentered the room wearing his typical jeans and chambray shirt. In his sock feet, he glanced down at the errant
boot hidden under the coffee table and nudged it out of
sight with his big toe. "She's a fine woman. And my
intentions are honorable. We aim to get married."

"But not too soon," Martha interjected. "We don't
want to take away from your wedding day."

Harold's solemn brown eyes shifted to Martha. He
walked over to his intended and put a supportive arm
around her waist. "Sorry, darlin', I know you wanted to
talk this over with Billie Rae privately, but I couldn't let
you face this alone."

Face this alone. The words were sweet and charming.
It was the support her mother needed. Tears stung Billie's
eyes with a mixture of relief, joy and sorrow. She'd had
to face so much alone: her father's death, then Jake's,
caring for the ranch and her mother. It was a comfort to
know someone else could take care of her mother now.
She felt overjoyed for them. She hadn't seen her mother
this happy in years.

But their blossoming love made her feel all the more
alone. A deep sorrow welled up inside her. Billie longed
for supportive arms to fold around her. She longed to
find one man she could truly love...and have it recipro-
cated. Squaring her shoulders, she knew she could survive...would have to survive without it. Because Nick
wasn't interested.

"If it makes you happy," she said, her throat tight with
too many emotions to catalog, "then I'm thrilled for you.
I really am." She sealed her approval with a sound kiss

to her mother's cheek and a warm hug for the fellow rancher.

Coughing into his hand, Harold stepped away from mother and daughter as they hugged again. "I don't know about you two, but a man could starve in this house."

"Oh, no, he couldn't." Martha laughed. "We'll feed you." She winked at Billie. "That is if you set the table, Harry."

His gaze snagged first on Martha then shifted to Billie for help. "I don't wanna break any of your dishes."

Billie smiled, her heart somehow feeling lighter. "Can't break any more than Jake used to. You have to get used to this household, we all chip in, even with cooking."

"Cooking?" The man swallowed hard.

"We won't make you do anything fancy at first. Maybe just grill a few steaks. But in the meantime, if it makes you more comfortable, use paper plates to set the table. They're in the cabinet over the fridge."

Harold frowned, and the two women shared a smile.

After a late breakfast of bacon, eggs and toast, Billie rose from the table, dumping her empty plate in the trash. "Thanks, Mom. It was delicious. Now I better go check out the damage. I've put it off long enough."

"I'm sure everything's fine," Harold said. "But I wish things had gone smoother between my son and your fiancé. He's not an easy man to work for. Of course, I taught my son not to be a quitter. But there's some times when a man's pride won't take any more."

A woman's, too, she thought. Doug wasn't an easy man to be engaged to, either. A frown pinched her brow. "How is your son? Doug told me he was kicked by a bull."

"Nothin' serious. But he's got a fair-size bruise to show for his trouble. He and your fiancé got off on the wrong foot, and they didn't see eye-to-eye on how to care for the cattle. So my boy got downright indignant. I hope you don't hold it against him."

"Not at all." She knew who was responsible for the trouble. "Send him over and I'll pay him for his troubles. If he's a mind to, I'll hire him. And this time, he'll work for me."

"That, I don't think he'd mind a bit." Harold wiped his mouth with a napkin and tossed it onto the table. "Thanks, darlin'." He kissed Martha's cheek. "That was mighty fine."

Awkward at seeing another man besides her father treat her mom in such a way, Billie chewed the inside of her lip. But the beaming smile on Martha's face made her relax. It suddenly felt like the old days, as if Jake and Nick would come racing through the back door, scaring up trouble and dust alike.

"You need any help down at the barn, Billie Rae?" Harold asked, pushing his chair under the table.

"Hold your horses, Harry." Martha hooked a dish towel over his shoulders. "There are pans to wash. I need a drier."

Smiling, Billie opened the back door and called over her shoulder, "Enjoy the morning. I'll be back later."

Ambling down to the barn, Billie felt her throat close with uncharted emotions. The twist of events over the past twenty-four hours set her mind to spinning. Seeing her mother so happy, and Harold Jacobson loving and caring for her, warmed Billie's heart and eased the ache over her own lost love.

Putting the many questions behind her, she threw herself into her work. She started with feeding the bulls, then checked on the heifers in the south pasture and took a turn through each of the other pastures. As she drove over her land, her family's land, she wondered if new changes were about to take place. Maybe Harold Jacobson could take over her duties. Maybe she didn't need a husband or his money. Maybe she could go to college on her own.

Satisfied the place hadn't fallen apart in the short time she'd been gone, she returned to the barn to feed Calamity and Diablo and muck out their stalls. The bucket rattled as she lifted it off the peg on the wall. With her motions set on automatic, she contemplated her future—with...or without Doug.

Before she had the first bucket of oats ready, she heard the roar of an engine. A minute later the soft tread of footsteps came toward her. She saw a shadow move along the wall. Her heart pummeled her chest cavity. Was it Nick? Was he coming for her? A rare, fervent hope leaped into her throat.

"So you're back, huh?" The caustic male voice snapped her out of her delusions.

"Yes, Doug." Irritation sharpened her tone. Dejection darkened her mood. "I'm back." Just as he'd requested.

His smug acceptance of her return grated on her. "Good."

"But I could use some help, since I got started late." She hid a sly grin by turning away from him. "You can muck out Diablo's stall." This would be a test.

"I didn't come down here this morning to work. I've got a meeting in forty minutes." He failed.

"Wouldn't want you to dirty up your loafers," she mumbled.

"What'd you say?"

"Nothing." She carried the bucket of rolled oats and grain into Calamity's stall, patted the mare and watched her nuzzle into her feed. "So what'd you come here for?"

"To make sure you'd returned, like I figured."

"Glad I met your expectations." Returning to the bins of feed, she scooped oats and molasses into the bucket for Diablo. Brushing past her fiancé, she headed toward the gelding's stall at the end of the row.

Doug put a hand on her arm, stopping her. "So what happened in Houston?"

Guilt trickled through her as Nick's kiss flared in her memory. "W-what do you mean?"

"I mean, what happened? Did you do any shopping? What'd you buy?"

Not in the mood to discuss her silly purchases, she edged past him, accidentally brushing the bucket against his trousers. "I don't have time for a social chat, Doug. I have chores. And you have work. Call me later."

He bent at the waist and rubbed at the dirty smudge the bucket left on his thigh. "I went to see Latham this morning."

That stopped her. Wrestling her jarred emotions back under control, she faced Doug again. Part of her wanted to shake him until his teeth rattled, until he told her every detail about Nick, what he'd said, how he'd looked. Had he mentioned her? What had he said? Had he appeared as tired she was? Did he have circles under his eyes like she did? Another part of her prayed Nick hadn't said a word about what had happened between them.

Or did she? Would that be an easy way out of her marriage? She suddenly realized she wanted a way out. Desperately.

"Why'd you go see him?" she asked, tense as a brittle limb.

"Work. He was closemouthed about your staying with

him. I don't think he even knew you'd come back here. Something weird seems to be going on. Was there something happening between you two?"

She refrained from answering that precise question. "Are you jealous?"

"Jealous of Nick Latham?" He laughed and a sliver of her heart broke off. "Not in the slightest."

Her ego felt scuffed by her fiancé's indifference and kicked by Nick. She realized she wanted Doug to be jealous, as Nick had been at the construction site. *As Nick had been.*

That thought made her pause, her hand on Diablo's stall door. Had Nick been jealous for a reason? Because he cared more than he wanted to admit?

The handle of the bucket bit into the palm of her hand. A low whiffling sound came from Diablo. She saw the gelding lift his back foot as if trying to paw the underside of his belly. Moving into the stall, she kept an eye on her brother's cantankerous horse and lifted the bucket to pour the feed into his narrow trough. She paused and looked closer.

"Did you already feed Diablo today?" she asked, nudging a good amount of feed pellets and rolled oats with her fingers.

"No." Doug stood outside the stall. "I just got here."

Scooping up a handful, she sniffed the leftover feed to see if she detected mildew or anything out of the ordinary. It seemed fine, so her attention switched to the gray gelding. Having been distracted earlier by thoughts of Nick, she hadn't noticed the horse's head drooped so low. He flicked his tail and stamped his back feet again. Concern filtered through her and erased all of her personal worries. "When did you last feed him?"

"I don't know."

She shot Doug an angry glance. "You don't know? Think. It's important." She rested a hand along Diablo's belly and the horse tried to shy away. She counted each breath, too rapid, too shallow. Her nerves tightened like a cinch. She remembered her conversation with Doug the previous night, remembered his sour contention that he didn't have to feed again. "Did you feed him last night, like you were supposed to?"

"Yeah. After I got off the phone with you.... I decided I better feed the stock again, since I wouldn't make it out here this morning. So they wouldn't go hungry. 'Cause I'm not as mean a guy as you made me out to be yesterday, I doubled their feed."

"You what?" She turned from Doug and studied Diablo with a practiced eye.

"What's the matter? He didn't eat it all."

"Because he's sick." Hot, angry, frightened tears pressed against the backs of her eyes. She forced them away with a hard swallow. She had to act fast. Her gaze scanned the stall, and she saw no fresh droppings. "Damn."

"I did like you said—"

"No, you didn't. Don't you understand? I left these animals in your care. They were your responsibility. I gave you specific instructions."

"Hell, the horse is just old."

Diablo buckled his front legs and started to lie down. "Oh, no, you don't," she said, hooking her arm under his neck and forcing the animal back to its feet. Over her shoulder she yelled, "Get me a halter and a rope. Now."

Amazingly, Doug followed her instructions. She told him how to make up a hot mash, while she kept Diablo calm and standing.

"What's wrong with him?" Doug asked, bringing the bucket of mash into the stall.

"It's got to sit for about ten minutes," she said, nodding that he could set it down and go.

"What is it?" he repeated.

"Colic."

"Isn't that what babies get?" he asked.

"Except this is life-threatening for a horse. He could die." Her throat burned and contracted with the painful thought. He wouldn't die. She wouldn't let him. "I can't let him lie down. He might try to roll to relieve the pain in his belly. He could twist a gut."

"All this because I doubled his feed?"

"Maybe. Horses have very delicate systems. It could be something else. He is old. He could have a blockage. Cancer...."

"Jeez, don't worry so much. He's bound to die sooner or later anyway. And then you won't have so many responsibilities. In fact, you ought to just sell all of them. It's not worth the time or effort. Just sell the whole lot of them. The herd, too."

"I can't believe what I'm hearing." Her brow slanted into a stern frown. "I'm not selling my cattle or my horses. I'm not going to just let this horse die to get rid of one of my responsibilities!"

"Why not? You don't want to be here anyway." His remark slapped her like a hand across the cheek. "Sell the livestock. And I'll turn this ranch into a moneymaking deal that can't lose."

Running a hand down Diablo's neck in slow, calming strokes, she flicked a disgusted look at Doug. "What did you have in mind?"

"A retirement center. So many folks are wanting to

leave Houston when they retire. Why not come out here?
We'll build a lake, set up home sites.''

''Is that why you went to see Nick in Houston? This
is already a plan you've put in motion?''

''Yeah. It'll make us a fortune.''

''And when were you going to tell me about this? After you'd broken ground?''

''Nah, I'd have told you after the wedding. You had
too much to think about before.'' He had a spark of confidence in his eye. ''I've already worked it out with a
building contractor. Talked to Nick today about handling
the roads and such. There will be a community golf
course, swimming pool, tennis courts, condos galore.
Babe, by the time you finish college, you'll be as rich as
Ivana Trump. Then you won't care anymore about being
a veterinarian. Then you can take your place by my side.
As my wife.''

She stared at him, her breathing as labored as Diablo's.
''Get off my land.''

''What?''

She shifted, getting a better grip on Diablo's halter. ''I
didn't work this long and this hard, just so I could sell
the ranch.''

''You don't have to sell, that's the beauty of this.''

''I'm not selling my livestock or selling out to you.
The wedding is off, Doug.''

''You can't do this!'' His face darkened. ''We made
an agreement. I've given my word to—''

''I don't care if you promised the pope. This is my
land. My family's land. I'm not selling out.'' She looked
away, more disgusted at herself than Doug. She should
have expected this from him. But she realized she'd really been no better than he. They'd both had their own
agendas. Now, at least, she knew for certain what his

was. "So this is why you wanted to marry me. I wondered. I wondered what a guy like you could see in a tomboy like me."

"Billie, it's not—"

"Yes, it is. Why do you think I wanted to marry you? I wanted to go to school, but keep the ranch running as it always has been. When I got my degree, I could practice here. I'd still have what my father worked his whole life to create, what Jake worked so hard to help me save. And I'd have my practice, what I'm good at."

Diablo dipped his head and shifted his feet, restless, like he wanted to lie down. But she couldn't let him. Edging him against the side of the stall, she leaned against his side, keeping a tight grip on his halter.

"I'm not stripping my land or destroying it with highrise condos or turning my pastures into a damn putting green. Not for you. Not for my own dreams. Not for any price."

"But—"

"You'll never own one blade of grass on this ranch." She reached for the bucket of mash and stuck it under Diablo's nose. "Come on, boy, eat some of this. You'll feel better."

Glancing at Doug over her shoulder, she said, "I'm sorry, Doug. The wedding's off. I can't marry you. We're too different. Now, go on home. You're not needed here anymore. I have work to do. A horse to try to save."

"Billie, can't I—"

"No, there's nothing else you can say." She turned to Diablo, hugged the gelding's neck and felt the hot tears seep out of her eyes and down her cheeks.

She'd gone on a wild, foolish chase for unreachable dreams. And in so doing, she'd risked the life of Harold Jacobson's son and this horse. She realized then that she'd been trying to have everything—her ranch, her career, a semblance of a marriage. But she should have learned a long time ago that she couldn't have everything she wanted. Life didn't work that way.

She could never have Nick. That simple fact crumpled the rest of her fragile composure.

Chapter Ten

"Billie Rae Gunther, you can't marry Doug Schaeffer!"

Nick's voice shook the rafters in the barn. He stalked through the wooden structure like a tiger on the prowl, looking into stalls until he found her with Diablo. The late evening sun slanted through the cracks in the wall, making the hay look ablaze with the amber glow and Billie's hair look like spun gold. "I won't let you make this damn-fool mistake."

Glancing up from her crouched position on the stall floor, Billie looked at him, her face grimy with sweat and streaked with dirt. Her blue eyes were red-rimmed and moist with unshed tears. A lone tear spilled over her lashes and rolled down her cheek. When had he ever seen her cry?

Immediately, Nick dropped to his knees beside her, his reason for coming forgotten, his heart pounding its way into his throat. "What's wrong?"

"Diablo." Her gaze shifted back to the horse lying on

the ground. She smoothed a hand along the horse's silvery mane. The gelding lay on its side, panting for breath.

"I don't think he's going to make it." Her voice cracked, and a chasm opened in his heart as he stared into her tortured face. "It's all my fault."

Resting his own hand on the horse's ribs, he ran his gaze down the length of the horse, noted the half-closed eyes, the shallow breathing. Nick's own heart beat wildly. He knew what this horse meant to Billie. It was Jake's. And her last link to her brother. A tightness clamped around his throat. What could he say to comfort her? What could he do to help her?

The horse shifted, lifting his legs and pawing the air.

"No!" Billie launched herself at the horse, flattening her body along its length, keeping it from rolling onto its back.

"What's wrong with him?" Nick asked, trying to help her ease the horse back onto its side but stay out of the way of Diablo's slashing hooves.

"Colic."

"Damn. When did it start?"

"Sometime this morning."

"Did you do a mash?"

She nodded. "He wouldn't eat much. Not enough to help."

"Call the vet?" Nick asked.

"Out of town. His assistant said he'd come out, but that I probably knew more than he did. And he's right. But I'm afraid I don't know enough." Desperation saturated her voice, making it a higher pitch that stabbed Nick right in the heart. "Nick, I'm not qualified for this. And he just keeps getting worse and worse. And it's all my fault. I should have never gone to Houston. I should have—"

He put a hand on her arm to stop her admission of guilt. This wasn't her fault. He couldn't believe that. Billie took better care of her stock than anyone. "Did he twist a gut?"

The tears stopped as suddenly as they'd started. She looked down at the gelding with a clinical eye. "I don't think so. He was standing when I found him. And it didn't look like he'd rolled yet. I couldn't keep him on his feet any longer, but I managed to keep him on his side."

"Good." His thumb smoothed along her forearm, the skin feeling sticky with sweat. "He is old, Billie. There may not be much of anything to do, vet or not."

Her spine stiffened. She glared at him. "Are you saying I should let him die?"

"Hell, no. But what I'm saying is it could be more than colic."

"I know." She sat back on her heels. "But his symptoms fit colic. Of course that could be only the start of a bigger problem. If it's cancer, then there's nothing anyone can do."

Solemn due to the circumstances, he nodded. "What can I do to help?"

She looked at him, her eyes filling with tears. "I don't know." Shifting her focus back to the gelding, she lifted his lip and checked the bluish color of his gums. "He's in shock. I don't know what else to do. Except a stomach wash."

"Do you have the equipment?"

"Yes, but I've never done it before."

"Diablo won't know."

She looked up at him, her blue eyes swimming with unshed tears. The stethoscope around her neck swayed.

"Let's do it, then."

He started rolling up his sleeves. "I'll help."

"I'm tired of this waiting." Billie crossed her arms over her chest, eyeing the gelding. He'd stopped grinding his teeth, working his jaw back and forth in a fruitless attempt to ease the pain in his belly. They'd forced Diablo to his feet, and he stood against the stall's side, his head drooping, as the fight seeped out of him. She'd finally given him a painkiller. Most vets recommended to wait so the symptoms wouldn't be masked. But she couldn't watch him suffer any longer.

She hurt for him, a raw ache opening in her chest. Her eyes felt gritty. But she couldn't have slept. She had to stay here and keep a watch. "There's nothing else we can do. Nothing!"

Helpless, she paced. What could she do? What had she missed? She couldn't operate. Not here. Not blindly. Not without the right instruments. Her frustration and uselessness crushed her. She felt totally alone in her grief.

Earlier, her mother had brought them sandwiches, had offered to assist. Harold had spent much of the afternoon offering support, giving advice. Now, as midnight closed in around them, her gaze shifted to Nick. He'd never left her side since he'd arrived like a whirling tornado earlier that day. She knew whatever happened, he'd stay with her. He'd help her see this through.

"Thanks, Nick, for everything." She nuzzled Diablo's neck, smelling the musty odor of his coat. She couldn't look Nick in the eye. Her emotions bubbled too close to the surface. If she looked directly at him, he'd see her love for him. "You've been a big help."

"I'm glad I was here." His voice somehow comforted her with its fullness. "Besides, it's nothing new. I've helped you before."

She nodded, a smile warming her as memories sifted over her. "I know. You helped me with that scrawny baby calf Dad found one winter. When was that? Your senior year?"

He nodded.

"It was half-dead. Dad wanted to put it down."

She heard Nick shifting behind her, his boots scooting the straw along the dirt floor. His low, warm chuckle soothed her frazzled nerves. "You put up some fight. Folks in Oklahoma probably heard your screeching. But you got him to agree you could try and save the poor calf."

"You stayed with me for three nights out at the barn. It was Christmas vacation, remember?" Needing to share this connection with Nick, she looked back at him. His smile created deep furrows in his cheeks, but she remembered the boy in him, the one reflected in his dark, liquid eyes. "We fed that calf every hour."

"You clocked our progress. Seemed like every time we managed to get a bottle down her, it was time to start again. But that calf made it. Thanks to you." His gaze shifted to Diablo, and hers followed.

She prayed the gelding would survive, too. There was nothing else they could do for him. "We can't lose him," she said, resolutely threading her fingers through his mane. "We can't. He's all I have left of Jake—" Her throat choked off the rest of her words, making her voice sound strangled. She leaned into the horse and wept for all the things she'd lost, for her father, her brother.

Nick's solid arms came around her and pulled her back against his chest. A warmth encased her, made her feel secure. "It's okay," he whispered. "I'll be here. No matter what happens."

But would he? Would he then turn and walk away as

he'd promised? Unable to love her as she needed? She continued crying, turning in the circle of his arms and snuffling against his shirt collar. He felt warm, solid and safe. But she knew, more than anything, she cried because she was losing Nick, too.

She let him hold her. With one arm secure around her, he took the lead rope into his own hand. Together, they kept watch over the horse. For the first time in years she felt connected, protected, cherished.

Watching the horse labor with each breath, fighting the inner demons that plagued him, Billie realized she'd been suffocating herself. Not with her dreams. But in not allowing herself to love.

She'd pushed Nick away when Jake died. It hadn't been fear of rejection. It had been fear of loss. She'd lost so much, so much, and she couldn't bear to lose any more. With each loss, a piece of her disappeared forever. What would be left of her if she lost Nick again?

As night closed in around them, she snuggled against Nick. If she lost Diablo, she'd need Nick's support. This time, she was woman enough to admit her need. She'd lost most of her family in the last few years. Was she willing to lose Nick, too?

Dawn arrived too bright and too damn early. Nick shifted on the hard-packed ground where he'd made himself as comfortable as possible. The first thing he saw was Billie, her face as radiant as the morning sun. She stood beside Diablo who munched on feed out of his trough. Nick grunted as he stood, his bones feeling cranky from sleeping on the hard-packed ground.

"He's going to make it, Nick." She came to him, wrapped her arms around his neck and kissed him soundly. The warmth of her lips pressed against his mouth woke him more than the sunlight peeking through the cracks. Surprised by her kiss and his own reaction, as his hands settled on her waist and pulled her closer against him, he kissed her right back.

"We did it." She laughed, tilting her face upward. "We really did."

He enjoyed the way she clung to him, the way she smiled up at him with joy and gratitude and... Was it love he saw shining in her blue eyes? He joined in her laughter, and for the first time his heart felt free of the constraints he'd belted around it.

He tightened his arms around her waist and pulled her against him, twirling her around and around until they stirred up a fair amount of dust motes from the straw. He dipped his head, nuzzled her neck and breathed in the sweet scent of her. She smelled like molasses and straw.

"So does that mean it's time to muck out the stall?" he asked.

She met his smiling eyes. "I think that'll be one chore I'll be happy to do. In fact, I don't think I'll ever dislike it again."

"So, Diablo's okay?"

"Better," she corrected. "His heart rate is normal. His breathing has slowed down. He's eating again and...everything associated with digesting his food seems to be working."

"Good." He held her tight, not ready to let her go, cherishing the moment. "See? You'll make a wonderful vet. You have to go to school, Billie."

"I don't know. I've realized how much I love it here," she said. "I'm not sure I can go off and leave it. Funny, huh? When that's exactly what I've been wanting to do for five years. Maybe I didn't want the choice taken away from me. I wanted it to be my decision to stay, not fate's." She shrugged. "I have so much to learn."

He shook his head. "You know what's most important." With her body pressed tight against him, he felt her heartbeat galloping and his beating in sync. He loved Billie, and it had taken almost losing her to another man for him to realize it. She'd been trying to love him for as long as he could remember. He'd pushed her away because he'd thought of her as a little sister, because he'd belonged to someone else, then because he hadn't really known how to love. But love came to Billie as natural as the sun rising in the east.

"You know how to love," he said, his voice cracking. How could he ever deserve her?

Had he waited too long to realize his own love? Did loving Billie mean he had to let her go…to pursue her own dreams? As much as he wanted to keep her, hold on to her, he knew she'd already made her choice. He wouldn't hold her back.

"Why'd you come back here?" she asked, stepping out of his arms. She studied him, from his tousled brown hair, his amber eyes to his rumpled shirt and jeans. A longing so strong and fierce welled up inside her that she knew she couldn't let Nick get away from her again.

"What?" he asked.

Her confidence growing with the assurance that he had kissed her back, really kissed her, she tried to control the smile that wanted to burst from her. "You came back here today, er, yesterday…for something. What was it?" She tapped her chin as if trying to remember, then she snapped her fingers. "Oh, yes, to stop the wedding. Again."

His gaze shifted away from her. He worked on

straightening his clothes and brushing his hair with his fingers. "Billie, we need to talk about Schaeffer."

"I'd rather not."

He jammed his hands into his back pockets and met her mischievous gaze. "There's something you need to know. I talked to Doug. He came to see me in Houston—"

"I know."

Surprise stole across his face. "He told you?"

She nodded. "Yep."

His jaw went slack, then his mouth thinned into a razor-sharp line. A tick hammered along the edge of his jaw. "Then you know? What he has planned?"

"Had. Had planned." She cast a glance at Diablo. The gelding ignored them and munched on fresh feed. She couldn't leave her stock, she couldn't sacrifice them, sell them or give up her ranch, for money...for anything. She loved this land, the place her father had built. And she wanted to keep it like a treasure. "Past tense." She faced Nick again. "I didn't know before yesterday what Doug had planned. But when I found out...I..."

She stopped explaining and took a step toward him. They could discuss the ranch later. They could discuss Doug much later. Right now, she needed to know why Nick had come back for her. Could he love her as she loved him? "Oh, no, you're on the hot seat now. Why'd you come here?"

"To tell you what Schaeffer had planned."

She took a step toward him. "And?"

"That's all." He shifted from boot to boot. His nervousness gave her courage that she'd never known before. Her newly discovered sixth sense told her she was on the right track.

"I don't think so." She moved closer, as if stalking him.

"That's all there is."

For a moment she hesitated, unsure of herself, unsure of Nick's feelings. But a strange glint in his eyes made her push harder. "Why do you care what I do with this ranch?"

He coughed into his hand and shifted from foot to foot. "Well, I've worked it. It's your family's. Your dad built it. Jake worked his butt off on it."

She shook her head, a grin lifting one corner of her mouth as certainty took hold of her heart. She stood toe-to-toe with him, and she wasn't going to let him wiggle out of the real reason he'd been so adamant to stop her wedding. "I don't buy it."

"Billie, look, you're going away soon to college."

"Yes," she said. "So?"

"You're getting married."

"Maybe...." Her eyes twinkled with mischief. "What about you?"

"Me?" He lifted a brow at that confusing statement. "I'm not very good at it."

"How do you know?"

His stomach dropped like a rock. "I'm divorced."

She frowned. "It takes two to make a successful marriage. Did you ever think you married the wrong woman?"

"Billie—"

"Nick, listen to me."

"Ah, hell." He hooked his arm around her waist and hauled her against his chest. He kissed her until her mind reeled and her heart almost stopped from the sheer joy. He kept right on kissing her until she wrapped her arms

around his neck and started to believe that Nick—*her*
Nick—Nicholas Barrett Latham, really cared for her.

"Dammit, Billie." He broke away. "What you do to
me."

"What's that?" she asked with a mysterious, feminine
smile.

"How did you make me fall in love with you?"

Her heart skipped a beat. Overwhelmed by his words,
she buried her face against his neck. She'd imagined him
saying that for so long, for so many lonely years. Hearing
it brought hot, blinding tears to her eyes.

"Billie? Billie? What'd I say? What'd I do now?"

"When did you figure this out?" she asked, her voice
muffled by his shirt.

"Last night. This morning. The first time I kissed you.
Hell, I don't know when, but I did. I fell hard for you."
He lifted her face so he could look into her eyes. "I need
you, Billie."

Still, doubting he felt for her what she felt for him, she
noted, "But you kissed me years ago."

Shaking his head, he chuckled. "You kissed me. Remember? Oh, I loved you back then, as a friend, as a
little sister. I didn't really know that you'd grown up. I
still thought of you as Billie the Kid with braces and
pigtails and black eyes. I didn't really know what love
was then, anyway.

"I'm talking about this week, though." His gaze
shifted to a distant spot, as if searching his memory. "Or
maybe it was when I heard you were getting married. Or
maybe you're right, maybe it was the first time we'd
kissed. Or maybe before that. Maybe I fell in love with
you down by Willow's Pond, sitting there sharing a fish-
ing pole as kids. Maybe it just took me till now to figure
it out."

Lifting her chin a notch, needing to know he had no delusions about who she was, she asked, "Do you think you could love a tomboy?"

She hated the quiver in her voice, the trembling in her limbs. But she had to know he could love her just as she was.

"Oh, Billie." His arms tightened around her, squeezing the very breath out of her. He kissed her, hard and fast, then slow and tender. It seemed as if she got lost in his kisses. And she didn't mind a bit.

"Yes, I love you." His voice sounded thick and deep with emotion. He kissed the tip of her nose. "I love your pert nose. I love the crease you get right here—" he kissed the furrowed skin between her brows "—when you're confused or angry at me. I love this mouth." He kissed her deeply, slipping his tongue inside and sweeping away all doubts. "I love *you*. As a tomboy, smelling like horses and cattle, as Billie the Kid, with dirt smudged across your brow." He wiped away a dirty smear across her forehead. "As a vet, with a need to help animals. And mostly as a Billie Rae Gunther, the beautiful woman you are. Someday, if I do my job, then you're going to believe that you are beautiful. Till then, I'm just going to have to keep telling you and keep showing you."

Her heart swelled, and blood hummed in her veins. "Oh, Nick. How much time we've wasted. I've loved you for so long…forever. Since I was a child, when I didn't even know what love was. I love you. I love the way you kiss me. I love the way you hold me. I love how you're always there for me, helping me, supporting me, encouraging me. I love that you wear jeans and boots. I love that you run your own company, your way. Nick Latham, I simply love all of you."

"So are you still going to marry that weasel Schaeffer? Or are you going to marry me?" he asked.

A smile tugged at the corner of her mouth. "I already called off the wedding. I was silly to think I could marry Doug without love. It couldn't have lasted. It was foolish. But I was desperate. I was so tired of life holding the reins. I wanted to be in control for once."

Nick kissed her once, twice, until they lost count. He pinched her chin between thumb and forefinger. "You didn't tell me your answer."

"Was that a proposal?" She quirked a brow at him.

"You mean…" His eyes widened.

She nodded.

"Never thought I'd ask a woman to marry me in a barn." He dropped to one knee and held her hand, turned it over and kissed her callused but tender palm. "Billie Rae Gunther, will you marry this man, who's not quite sure how to love you, but wants to do his damnedest?"

Standing in her faded jeans and filthy shirt, she said, "Yes, Nicholas Barrett Latham, I would be most honored to be your bride."

He stayed on his knees, looking up at her, love making his brown eyes look like liquid pools. Slowly she sank to her knees and met his gaze squarely. Their breaths mingled, merged into one, as soon their bodies would.

"Aren't you going to kiss me?" she asked impatiently.

"I'm going to do a whole lot more than that." He settled her snug against him, chest to chest, hips against hips. She felt his hardness press against her, showing her how much he desired her. "But first I have one more question."

She pushed against his shoulders to get a better look at him. "What's that?"

"Did you really buy that nightgown for Schaeffer's benefit?"

A blush burned her cheeks like the sunrise setting fire to the horizon. "I was thinking of you when I picked it out."

He gave her a devilish grin. He pushed to his feet, then lifted her into his arms. "Then you can wear it for me on our honeymoon."

"Where are you taking me?" she asked, breathless.

"Someplace with more privacy."

She glanced over his shoulder at Diablo. The gelding gave her a parting glance then turned to get some water. For the first time in her life, she felt accepted and loved for herself, like a blushing bride. Then Nick kissed Billie, like a real woman should be kissed. And she understood what her mother meant about falling in love and passion carrying you away.

* * * * *

Leanna Wilson sure does love Texas!
Look for ARE YOU MY DADDY? this November
from Silhouette Romance. It tells the story of one
Fabulous Father!

HERE COME THE
Virgin Brides!

Celebrate the joys of first love with more unforgettable stories from Romance's brightest stars:

SWEET BRIDE OF REVENGE
by Suzanne Carey—June 1998 (SR #1300)

Reader favorite Suzanne Carey weaves a sensuously powerful tale about a man who forces the daughter of his enemy to be his bride of revenge. But what happens when this hard-hearted husband falls head over heels...for his wife?

THE BOUNTY HUNTER'S BRIDE
by Sandra Steffen—July 1998 (SR #1306)

In this provocative page-turner by beloved author Sandra Steffen, a shotgun wedding is only the beginning when an injured bounty hunter and the sweet seductress who'd nursed him to health are discovered in a remote mountain cabin by her gun-toting dad and *four* brothers!

SUDDENLY...MARRIAGE!
by Marie Ferrarella—August 1998 (SR #1312)

RITA Award-winning author Marie Ferrarella weaves a magical story set in sultry New Orleans about two people determined to remain single who exchange vows in a mock ceremony during Mardi Gras, only to learn their bogus marriage is the real thing....

And look for more VIRGIN BRIDES in future months, only in—

Silhouette ROMANCE™

Available at your favorite retail outlet.

Look us up on-line at: http://www.romance.net   SRVBJ-A

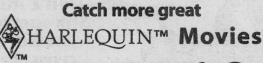

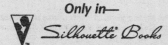

In **July 1998** comes

THE MACKENZIE FAMILY

by *New York Times* bestselling author

LINDA HOWARD

The dynasty continues with:

Mackenzie's Pleasure: Rescuing a pampered ambassador's daughter from her terrorist kidnappers was a piece of cake for navy SEAL Zane Mackenzie. It was only afterward, when they were alone together, that the real danger began....

Mackenzie's Magic: Talented trainer Maris Mackenzie was wanted for horse theft, but with no memory, she had little chance of proving her innocence or eluding the real villains. Her only hope for salvation? The stranger in her bed.

Available this July for the first time ever in a two-in-one trade-size edition. Fall in love with the Mackenzies for the first time—or all over again!

Available at your favorite retail outlet.

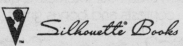

Silhouette Books

The World's Most Eligible Bachelors are about to be named! And Silhouette Books brings them to you in an all-new, original series....

World's Most Eligible Bachelors

Twelve of the sexiest, most sought-after men share every intimate detail of their lives in twelve never-before-published novels by the genre's top authors.

Don't miss these unforgettable stories by:

Dixie Browning

MARIE FERRARELLA

Jackie Merritt

Tracy Sinclair

BJ James

RACHEL LEE

Suzanne Carey

Gina Wilkins

VICTORIA PADE

MAGGIE SHAYNE

Anne McAllister

Susan Mallery

Look for one new book each month in the
World's Most Eligible Bachelors series beginning
September 1998 from Silhouette Books.

✌ Silhouette ®

Available at your favorite retail outlet.

International bestselling author

JOAN JOHNSTON

continues her wildly popular Hawk's Way miniseries with an all-new, longer-length novel

THE SUBSTITUTE GROOM

HAWK'S WAY

August 1998

Jennifer Wright's hopes and dreams had rested on her summer wedding—until a single moment changed everything. Including the *groom*. Suddenly Jennifer agreed to marry her fiancé's best friend, a darkly handsome Texan she needed—and desperately wanted—almost against her will. But U.S. Air Force Major Colt Whitelaw had sacrificed too much to settle for a marriage of convenience, and that made hiding her passion all the more difficult. And hiding her biggest secret downright impossible…

"Joan Johnston does contemporary Westerns to perfection." —*Publishers Weekly*

Available in August 1998
wherever Silhouette books are sold.